SONS OF

The
PRINCE

a novella

ENCOURAGEMENT

FRANCINE RIVERS

TYNDALE HOUSE PUBLISHERS, INC.
WHEATON, ILLINOIS

Library of Congress Cataloging-in-Publication Data

Rivers, Francine, date.
 The prince / Francine Rivers.
   p. cm. — (Sons of encouragement ; 3)
 ISBN-13: 978-0-8423-8267-0 (hc)
 ISBN-10: 0-8423-8267-4 (hc)
  1. Jonathan (Biblical character)—Fiction.   2. Bible. O.T.—History of Biblical events—Fiction.   3. David, King of Israel—Fiction.   I. Title.
 PS3568.I83165P754 2005
 813'.54—dc22

                                                                          2005011961

Printed in the United States of America

10   09   08   07   06   05
9   8   7   6   5   4   3   2   1

To men of faith who serve
in the shadow of others.

+ + +

FROM the beginning of my writing career, my husband, Rick, has blessed me continually with his encouragement. Without him, I might not have had the courage to send in the first manuscript that began my journey as a writer. He listens to my ideas, makes space for me in his office at Rivers Aviation, brews great coffee, and edits the final draft. He even builds me a fire on cool mornings.

The Lord has also blessed me with encouraging friends. I want to mention two in particular: Peggy Lynch and Pastor Rick Hahn. I can't even count the number of times I've called Peggy or Pastor Rick to ask where a Scripture passage is and/or to check my understanding of God's Word. Both of these friends have loved Jesus since childhood, have a passion for God's Word, and are gifted teachers. Each played an important part in bringing my husband and me to Jesus, and each continues to teach and encourage us in our walk with the Lord today. May the Lord bless you for your kindness!

I want to thank my editor, Kathy Olson, and Ron Beers for their continued support and encouragement. I greatly appreciate their willingness to work with me to strengthen each story. There are so many people at Tyndale who have encouraged and prayed for me over the years. From the beginning of our relationship, I have felt part of the team.

And I want to thank all those who have prayed for me over the years and through the course of this particular project. When I'm assailed by doubts, which often happens, I remember you are praying. May the Lord bless each of you for your tender hearts.

May Jesus Christ be glorified in this story that came from His Word. May each reader be encouraged to love the Lord with heart, mind, soul, and strength and to walk in His ways daily. Jesus is life abundant and everlasting. Blessed be the name of the Lord.

DEAR READER,

This is the third of five novellas on biblical men of faith who served in the shadows of others. These were Eastern men who lived in ancient times, and yet their stories apply to our lives and the difficult issues we face in our world today. They were on the edge. They had courage. They took risks. They did the unexpected. They lived daring lives, and sometimes they made mistakes—big mistakes. These men were not perfect, and yet God in His infinite mercy used them in His perfect plan to reveal Himself to the world.

We live in desperate, troubled times when millions seek answers. These men point the way. The lessons we can learn from them are as applicable today as when they lived thousands of years ago.

These are historical men who actually lived. Their stories, as I have told them, are based on biblical accounts. For the facts we know about the life of Jonathan, see the books of 1 and 2 Samuel.

This book is also a work of historical fiction. The outline of the story is provided by the Bible, and I have started with the information provided for us there. Building on that foundation, I have created action, dialogue, internal motivations, and in some cases, additional characters that I feel are consistent with the biblical record. I have attempted to remain true to the scriptural message in all points, adding only what is necessary to aid in our understanding of that message.

At the end of each novella, we have included a brief

study section. The ultimate authority on people of the Bible is the Bible itself. I encourage you to read it for greater understanding. And I pray that as you read the Bible, you will become aware of the continuity, the consistency, and the confirmation of God's plan for the ages—a plan that includes you.

Francine Rivers

ONE

"**WE** have no weapons!"

"We'll have to find a way to make them."

"How? There isn't a blacksmith in the whole land of Israel to make them. The Philistines made sure of that. Those they didn't murder, they took captive."

Jonathan sat with his father, Saul, beneath the shade of an olive tree. His uncles, frustrated and angry, bewailed the latest Philistine raid.

"Even if we could make swords, what good would they be? Whatever the Philistines' swords and spear tips are made of, they're far superior to ours. Bronze isn't strong enough. It shatters against their blades."

"I choke on my pride every time I have to go down to Aijalon and pay hard-earned shekels to a stinking Philistine so he'll sharpen my plowshare and sickles!"

"If I need an ax sharpened, I have to answer question after question."

Another laughed bitterly. "I need my pitchfork repaired this year, and new points for the ox goad. I wonder how much that will cost me."

Saul stared off toward the fields. "There's nothing we can do about it."

The Philistine outpost at Geba was only a short distance away, and it was the duty of Saul's tribe, the Benjaminites, to keep close watch over it.

"Kish says what we need is a king!"

Saul shook his head. "You know what the prophet Samuel says about having a king."

"The Philistines have kings. That's why they're organized."

"If only Samuel were like Samson. Instead, all he does is blame us for what's happening."

Jonathan looked at his father. "Grandfather Ahimaaz said the Lord our God is more powerful than all the gods of Philistia."

The uncles exchanged sallow looks.

Jonathan leaned forward. "Grandfather Ahimaaz said when the Philistines killed the high priests' sons and took the Ark of the Covenant, God went to war against them. Their god Dagon fell facedown before the Ark, his head and the hands breaking off. And then the Lord cursed the Philistines with tumors and a plague of rats. They were so afraid they sent the Ark back on a cart pulled by two milch cows and loaded with gold!"

Saul shook his head. "That was years ago."

One of Jonathan's uncles flung a pebble. "God leaves us alone now to defend ourselves."

Jonathan felt confused. "But if the Lord—"

Saul looked at him. "Your mother tells you too many stories about what her father said."

"But they're true, aren't they?"

Another uncle snorted in despair. "It was years ago! When was the last time the Lord did anything for us?"

Saul put his arm around Jonathan. "There are things you don't yet understand, my son. When you are a man—"

"*Saul!*"

At the sound of Kish's angry shout, Saul removed his arm from around Jonathan's shoulders and stood. "What now?" he grumbled. "I'm here!"

Jonathan's grandfather strode across the partially

plowed field, his fine robes billowing around him, the red tinge in his cheeks betraying his temper. His younger sons scattered like chaff before a strong wind, leaving Saul alone to face their father.

Saul came out from the shade. "What's the matter?"

His question fanned the flames. "What's the matter? You have to ask me?"

Saul's face darkened. "If I knew, I wouldn't ask."

"You're out here sitting in the shade, and my donkeys are missing!"

"Missing?" Saul frowned and looked off toward the hills.

"Yes! Missing! Have you no ears that you can hear?"

"I told Mesha to watch over the donkeys."

Jonathan gulped. Mesha was an old man, easily distracted. No wonder the donkeys had gone missing.

"Mesha?" Kish spat in disgust. "Mesha!"

Saul spread his hands. "Well, I can't be in two places at the same time. I've been plowing the field."

"Plowing? Is that what you call sitting under an olive tree, talking with your brothers?" Kish shouted for the rest to hear. "Will we have enough food with all of you sitting around talking?"

"We were making plans."

"Plans for what?"

"War."

Kish barked a harsh laugh. "We would need a king to lead us into war, and we have no king. Where are my donkeys?" He made a fist.

Saul stepped back out of range of a blow. "It's not my fault Mesha didn't do as he was told!"

"You'll lose the oxen next! How long do you think

you'll manage without animals to pull the plow? I'll have to put *you* to harness!"

Saul's face reddened. He stalked back into the shade.

Kish followed. "I put you in charge! I didn't want a servant watching over my donkeys! I wanted *my son* watching them!"

"You have more than one son!"

"You're the eldest!" He cursed. "Mesha is an old man and a hireling. What does it matter to him if my property is lost? You're the one to inherit. If you had to put someone over those animals, why didn't you send Jonathan? He would have kept close watch over my property."

Jonathan cringed. Why did his grandfather have to pitch him into the fray? His father's pride was easily pricked.

Saul glared. "You always blame me when anything goes wrong!"

"Father, I'll go look—"

"No, you won't!" both men shouted.

"I'll send one of the servants." Saul turned as if to leave.

Kish yelled, "No, you won't! You'll go yourself. And don't give me excuses! You're not going to sit out here on your backside and wait for someone else to find what you allowed to wander off. Take a servant with you, and go look for the donkeys!" Kish strode back toward Gibeah, still shouting. "And don't even think about riding a donkey. There's only one donkey left, and that one stays here. You can search on foot! And take someone other than *Mesha* with you!"

Saul kicked the dust and muttered. Eyes blazing, he stormed across the field toward home. Jonathan followed.

His mother, Ahinoam, stood in the doorway, waiting for them. The whole town had probably heard Kish shouting out in the field. "I've filled two water bags and stuffed two packs with bread."

His father scowled. "You're so eager to have me go?"

She put her hand against his heart. "The sooner you go, the sooner you will be back."

"I'll go with you, Father."

Ahinoam followed Saul inside the house. "Jehiel knows more about donkeys than any man in Gibeah, Saul. Take him with you. Jonathan can continue the plowing."

"But, Mother—"

She gave Jonathan a quelling look. "With both of you gone, nothing would get done."

"Father, the Philistines may have stolen the donkeys and taken them to Geba." The garrison was not far away. "We should go there first."

His mother faced him. "You're not going. Your father has enough to do without having to watch out for you."

Jonathan's face went hot. "I can use a bow better than any man in Gibeah."

"Your father is going out to find donkeys, not start a war."

"Enough!" Saul snarled. "Pack me enough bread and dried fruit to last me a few days. There's no telling how far the donkeys have wandered."

His wife moved quickly to do his bidding.

Saul muttered and stormed around the room, kicking things out of his way. When he saw Jonathan still standing there, he jerked his chin. "Go and find Jehiel. Tell him to hurry up!"

"I'll go." Jonathan backed toward the door. "But what if the donkeys are in Geba?"

Saul flung his hand into the air. "Then they're gone, aren't they? And Mesha will wish he had done what he was told!"

"They've wandered off." Ahinoam spoke in soothing tones. "That's all that's happened. You'll find them before the sun sets, my love." She shoved more bread into a sack. "The Philistines have more donkeys than they need. Besides, they covet horses."

Saul shouted after Jonathan. "Tell Jehiel I'm ready and waiting on him!"

Jonathan found Jehiel hard at work repairing the wall of an empty sheepfold. "Kish is sending my father out to find some stray donkeys. My father wants you to go with him. He's packed and ready to go."

Jehiel straightened and brushed his hands off. "I will gather what I need and come."

Jonathan followed him. "You could tell my father that the sheep might escape if you don't complete your work. You could say I can serve him as well as you." He had explored the hills and valleys all around Gibeah and even dared go close enough to the walls of Geba to hear the guards talking.

"The sheep are out to pasture, Jonathan, and there are two shepherds to watch over them."

"What if you run into Philistines while you're searching for the donkeys?"

"You needn't worry about your father. We will avoid the Philistines. Even if by mischance we crossed paths with them, I doubt they would bother with two men on foot with little more than some bread and water to steal."

Jonathan sighed.

Before the two men left, Saul gripped Jonathan's shoulder. "Finish plowing the west field. Keep watch over your brothers. You know how they tend to wander."

"I wish I were going with you."

Saul looked past him to Ahinoam. "Soon."

✦   ✦   ✦

Jonathan went out to work in the west field. Not long after his father and Jehiel had left, his mother came out to him. It was not her habit to do so, and he stopped the oxen to wait. "Is something wrong?"

"No. Nothing. Sit with me in the shade and rest a while."

"Father wanted me to plow—"

"I will not keep you from your work for long, my son."

He secured the reins and followed her. She led him to the same tree where he had sat earlier with his father and uncles, listening to talk of kings and war.

Kneeling, she laid out fresh bread, a skin of wine, dried dates and raisins.

Jonathan's brows rose slightly. Perhaps she meant to sweeten words that would sour his mood. His defenses rose.

She looked up at him. "You are still upset that you weren't allowed to go with your father."

"These are troubled times, Mother, and he is too important a man to be guarded by only one servant. What if they meet some Philistines?"

"Your father is looking for donkeys, not a fight."

Women would never understand! "You don't have to look for a fight to find yourself in the middle of one."

His mother sighed. "You love your father, Jonathan. In that, I know your heart is ever in the right place. But you must learn to use your head, my son. I saw you stand and watch your father and Jehiel depart. Did they head for the garrison? Did they go armed to accuse and ready to fight?" She folded her hands in her lap. "You would have urged your father to look in Geba first. Would that be in keeping with protecting your father, or urging him to danger?"

"But that's probably where the donkeys are."

"Just because a lamb is missing doesn't mean it's in a lion's mouth. Jehiel will try to track the donkeys. We can hope the Philistines had nothing to do with them. If they did, then they're gone and that's the end of it."

Jonathan rubbed his face in frustration. "The Philistines take everything they can get their hands on."

"I did not come out here to talk about Philistines or donkeys. God knows where the donkeys are. And if it is God's will, He will let your father find them. I care more about my son than a few beasts of burden." She stood and squeezed his hand. "I came out to tell you I am very proud of you, Jonathan. You have courage. I just want you to live long enough to have good sense."

She leaned down and covered the bread with a cloth. "If all Israel has its way, we will soon have a king like every other nation around us. And what else does a king do but draft sons into the army or make them run before his chariot? Your sisters may one day end up cooks or bakers or perfumers in some palace in Judah's territory, since Judah thinks it must be one of their own rather than a Benjaminite to rule. A king will take the best of our crops and herds and give them to his assistants. He will want a portion of everything we have. These are the things the prophet Samuel told your grandfather and the others who went to Ramah to ask for a king. Samuel speaks the truth. All you have to do is look around you to see—"

"We are at the Philistines' mercy, Mother. Would you have us sit and do nothing?"

"My father, Ahimaaz, was a great man. He said we must trust in the Lord. God is our king."

"God has abandoned us."

"Men who say such things have no faith, and without faith, we have no hope." His mother raised her hands in frustration. "I know, I am but a woman. What could I know?" She raised her chin, dark eyes sparkling. "But I do know that you are my son. You are the grandson of Ahimaaz. Listen to *his* words, not mine. If a man is going to follow God, he must align himself with men of God. Samuel is God's anointed prophet. He speaks God's Word. Listen carefully to what *he* says."

"I wasn't in Ramah." How did she know so much of what was said there?

"I wish you had been. You'd have heard for yourself the words of the prophet rather than hearing your mother repeat what she overheard." She sighed. "I came to say that many things could change and it could happen quickly. While you work in the fields, pray. Ask the Lord what He requires of you."

And what did the Lord want of him but to fight, to drive the idol worshipers from the land?

His mother studied him. Her eyes darkened and grew moist. She shook her head slowly, rose, and walked away.

+   +   +

A day passed, then another, and Jonathan's father and
Jehiel did not return. His mother said nothing.

The men gathered at Kish's table and complained about
the Philistines; then complained about Samuel's corrupt
sons, who were now assigned to rule over Israel. Jonathan
sat with his younger brothers—Malkishua, Abinadab, and
Ishbosheth—and ate in silence, worrying about his father.

Saul's cousin Abner cut off a portion of roasted goat.
"Samuel was not pleased when we met with him at Ramah.
He took our request for a king as a personal affront."

Kish dipped bread into the bowl of lentil stew. "He is
not long for this world, and we need a man to rule before
he goes the way of all flesh. There are none like Samuel in
the land."

"All too true! But his sons are despicable."

"They hold court in Beersheba and collect tribute like
pagan kings!"

One of Jonathan's uncles reached for a cluster of grapes.
"They have been helpful in the past."

Kish gave a harsh laugh. "Only because we paid them
larger bribes than those who complained against us! Joel
and Abijah cannot be trusted. They are greedy and will
turn their rulings to whomever gives them what they
want."

"And what they want changes from one day to the
next."

"How does a man like Samuel come to have sons like
those two?"

"Kish, you convinced Samuel, didn't you, my brother?
He said we would have a king."

Kish poured wine. "The question is when? And who will it be? A Judean? So it will be, according to Jacob's prophecy."

"There is not a Judean worthy enough to rule over us!"

"Why not you, Kish? You are rich."

Kish's brothers and sons, equally ambitious for the tribe of Benjamin, were quick to agree.

"You are a leader of Israel."

"The greatest among all the tribes."

"You have influence."

"The other tribes grumble, but it is clear their elders look to our house to rule."

Kish's dark eyes glowed with fire. "I know they look to us, but I am an old man. It will take someone younger and stronger than I, a man of stature who will impress the other tribes enough to convince them to stand behind him."

Jonathan leaned in to listen. There was no man taller nor of more regal bearing than his father, Saul.

"The twelve tribes must be unified. We need a king like the nations around us, a champion who will go out and fight for us."

Jonathan thought of his mother's words about Ahimaaz. Ahimaaz had been killed by Philistines, and Jonathan had few memories of him, other than that he had not been like Kish. Kish was angry. Loud. Always making plans for war. Ahimaaz had taught Jonathan to say, "Trust in the Lord and the power of His strength." Kish believed God helped those who helped themselves. And Kish ruled the men gathered in this room. They all believed that the Lord had left them to protect themselves, and to stand against the Philistines meant they must adopt the ways of the nations around them, nations who had powerful kings and large armies. Some even thought the gods of Philistia were more powerful than the God of Abraham, Isaac, and Jacob. How else could they be so oppressed by the Philistines?

Kish tore off another piece of bread. "Samuel said God will give us what we want."

Every man in the room knew who Kish had in mind. The men had talked often among themselves. Saul stood a head taller than any other man in Gibeah, and he had the famed handsome features of the Benjaminite tribe, descended from the youngest son of Jacob's beautiful and favored wife, Rachel. Men—and women—stared every time Saul attended one of the religious festivals, not that he attended often. He would rather plow, plant, and harvest crops than attend religious services, even though he was required to go three times a year. Saul *looked* like a king even if he had no ambitions to become one.

Jonathan knew it didn't matter what Kish wanted. God would tell Samuel whom to choose.

As much as he loved and respected his father, he could not imagine Saul as king.

But if not Saul, who? Abner? He was an able leader, fierce and uncompromising. Or Amasa, Abner's brother? Both were men of courage and strength, always talking over plans of how they would drive the Philistines from the land if God would just give them a king to pull the tribes together. They could talk, but could they lead?

Jonathan looked around at his relatives. They were all eager for a king, intent upon having one whether Samuel liked it or not. If his father were made king, it would change everything. Jonathan felt a rush of apprehension at the thought that he would then become the heir to the throne.

His mother's words pricked his spirit: *"Trust in the Lord. He is our king."*

Then why didn't the Lord destroy their enemies? Why did He allow the Philistines to oppress them? If God still cared, why didn't He deliver them? He had sent Moses. He had sent others. Every now and then, it seemed the Lord awakened to their need and sent a man to deliver them. But years had passed and no one had come. The only Word they had from God came through Samuel, who said they were at fault.

What was left, then, but for every man to do what was right in his own eyes? For it was certain no one had confidence in Samuel's sons to make decisions with the wisdom and justice of their father.

Jonathan had heard Samuel speak only once, but still remembered how his heart had quickened when the prophet reminded the people how their forefathers had been slaves in Egypt, and how God had sent Moses to deliver them from bondage. God had sent the plagues to free them from Pharaoh, had given the people water in the desert, and rained manna from heaven. God had opened the Red Sea to save Israel and then closed it over Pharaoh's army. Whatever the people needed, God had provided. All the years they wandered in the wilderness and suffered under the blazing desert sun, they had water and food enough. Their shoes and clothing never wore out. When all those who had refused to trust in the Lord died, their children crossed the River Jordan and claimed the land God promised. Canaan, a land of milk and honey.

Samuel said the Lord their God had driven out many of

the Canaanites before they came, and then commanded His people to drive out the rest. The Lord had tested them to see if they would follow His commandments with single-minded determination. As long as Joshua, then Caleb, then Othniel lived, they had obeyed. But eventually, the people had grown tired of fighting and had given up trying to wipe the land clean. So what if a few enemies survived in caves and crags? God's people had tried, hadn't they? Surely God couldn't expect more of them than that. It was too much work to hunt the stragglers down and finish them off. What harm to leave them alone? It was time to enjoy the crops, the flocks and herds, the fruit trees ready for harvest. It was time to savor the milk and honey!

But the surviving enemy had been like weeds. They grew quickly and spread.

And now, here were the Philistines—a garrison of them—only a few hills away. These people from the sea were powerful, armed, and arrogant. And they moved farther inland every year. No one in Israel did anything to drive them from the land. No one dared, especially now that not a single blacksmith could be found to forge a weapon. And how could twelve disparate tribes with countless leaders unite and fight against the organized forces that moved beneath the command of a king?

"We need a king like they have. Without a king to unite us, we are defenseless."

"When a king unites us, we won't have to live in fear, wondering from one day to the next whether marauders are going to steal our crops and animals."

Animals!

Jonathan felt a rush of fear. His father had not yet returned. How long did it take to find a few donkeys?

God, please bring my father home safely.

Did God even hear their prayers anymore? *Had* the Lord abandoned them, as some of his relatives claimed? Did the Lord expect them to live by their own strength and cunning?

Samuel said if they returned to the Lord, the Lord would deliver them from their enemies. But Jonathan didn't understand what the prophet meant. How had he left the Lord? The Philistines continued to encroach bit by bit, taking more territory, striking at every weak place, building strongholds. And God did not stop them. He did not intervene and sweep His mighty hand across the land, even though from history, Jonathan knew it would be a small thing for the God who sent ten plagues upon Egypt to send another plague or two upon the Philistines! Why didn't He?

His mother had told him that his grandfather Ahimaaz used to say, "Every trial that comes will strengthen or weaken our faith."

The Philistines increased in number and power every year. They dressed in their fine-colored garments and armor, their thick hair like braided crowns, heads high, armed to kill, quick with mocking laughter and unleashed passion before their idols. They were a sight to see! Did their gods exist? How else did they come by such confidence in themselves and disdain for others? They were the conquerors, making themselves rich off those they oppressed. Israel was stripped while God remained silent.

"The Lord has spoken to Samuel and told him a king will be chosen." Kish put his wine goblet down. "Either he agrees that we need a king, or he no longer plans to rule."

Did Kish mean God or Samuel? Either way, Jonathan felt a chill spread through his blood.

Could his father or any other man effectively rule Israel? Whenever the elders gathered, they bickered. They might believe in God, but they distrusted one another.

Jonathan's mind wandered.

What must it have been like to live beneath God's protection—the cloud by day, the pillar of fire by night? What had the manna tasted like? What must it have felt like to see water streaming from a rock? Jonathan often yearned for days he had never experienced. He felt bereft, soul starved.

He used to dream of studying the Law—perhaps even at Naioth, where Samuel was. The Lord spoke to Samuel. Samuel would know the answers to the questions that often plagued Jonathan. What did it mean to trust and obey God? What action should he take to please Him? Clearly, the offerings did not suffice. God was far off, silent. Did the Lord listen to anyone other than Samuel?

As great a man as Samuel was, as honest and upright a judge, he paled next to stories of Moses, who had brought the Law down from Mount Sinai, and Joshua, who had conquered the land. Those had been days when God ruled as king! God had gone out ahead of them in battle and stood as their rear guard. He had hurled hailstones from heaven! Who could stand against a God like that? He had made slaves into free men and frightened sheep into an army of lions.

But where was the army of Israel now? The mighty warriors who once claimed their inheritance had produced frightened sheep that bleated over scant crops and drying water holes, and lived in fear of Philistine wolves.

What if Kish got what he wanted and lived to see Saul crowned king over Israel? Jonathan felt a rush of fear. His father was a farmer, not a warrior. Even now, he might be dead. It should not have taken this long to find the donkeys.

Jonathan gave voice to his concern. "My father has been gone too long. Can I go and look for him?"

Abner frowned. "Saul *has* been gone a long time."

Kish considered for a moment, then waved his hand. "It is too early to be concerned, my son."

"He's been gone two full days, Grandfather."

Kish gave a bleak laugh. "One day to find the donkeys, one day to sulk, one day to return. If he hasn't come home by the day after tomorrow, then I will worry."

"With your permission, I will go and look for him tomorrow. He could have run into trouble."

"The boy thinks he could take on some Philistines."

Jonathan was thirteen and a man. How long before they saw him as such?

"Be quiet. Should we dismiss a son's love for his father?" Kish's eyes glowed with pride as he studied Jonathan, but he shook his head. "Your father takes his time because he is angry. He'll be home in a few days."

Jonathan wished he could be as certain.

✦   ✦   ✦

Jonathan heard the cry of alarm. One of the shepherds came running across the field. "The donkeys are at the well."

Something must have happened to his father! Jonathan took off running. "Grandfather!"

Kish came out. Jonathan told him about the donkeys,

and Kish shouted to the shepherd, "Have you seen my son?"

"No, my lord. I've seen no sign of him."

"Let me go." Jonathan feared they had waited too long already. "Let me go find my father!"

Kish shouted and several men came running.

Jonathan refused to be set aside. "I have to go!"

"Abner will go."

"Let me go with him."

Kish grabbed hold of Jonathan's shoulder. "Go! But do not look for trouble."

They traveled quickly, stopping to ask if anyone had seen Saul and Jehiel. They had been seen, but had gone on. Jonathan and Abner passed through the hill country of Ephraim, through the area around Shalishah, and on into the district of Zuph, following word of them.

Abner looked perplexed. "The seer lives here."

Would his father come all this way to ask Samuel where the donkeys were?

Eyes glowing, Abner entered the town of Naioth. "We'll have news of Saul here. I'm certain of it."

Yes, Saul and his servant had been there. The town was still talking about him.

"Samuel invited Saul to eat with him." Men were still talking about the feast. "Samuel had saved the best portion of the lamb for him."

The best portion? What did that mean? "Why?"

"We don't know, but Samuel seemed to be expecting him."

Jonathan looked around. "Where is my father now?"

"Gone."

Abner's voice was strained with excitement. "What of Samuel? May we speak with him?"

"He left as well."

"Did they leave together?" Abner wanted to know.

One elder shrugged while the other pointed. "No. Saul took the road to Bethel."

Abner grasped Jonathan's arm. "Let's go. We must hurry!"

"What do you think happened?"

"We'll find out when we find your father."

Saul and Jehiel were not in Bethel. Apparently Saul and his servant had entered the town with three others, were given bread, and had taken the road to Gibeah.

"Maybe he found out the donkeys came back," Jonathan said.

Abner laughed strangely. "Or maybe something else!"

They came upon others who had seen Saul and were full of news about what had happened.

"Your father joined the procession of prophets coming down from the high place in Gibeah. He prophesied with them!"

Jonathan's father, a prophet? How could that be?

Others came near to hear what was being said.

"What happened to the son of Kish?"

"He prophesied!"

"What? Is even Saul a prophet?"

Jonathan pressed in among them. "Where is my father now?"

"He's gone up to the high place!"

But by the time they got there, Saul and Jehiel were gone.

"How long ago did they leave?"

"Not long."

Jonathan and Abner ran to catch up. Finally, Jonathan spotted a tall man and a smaller one walking beside him on a distant hill. "Father!" Jonathan shouted and increased his speed. Abner was on his heels.

Saul turned and waited. He embraced Jonathan, pounded him on the back, and grinned.

"We were worried about you and came looking." Jonathan panted. What was that he smelled on his father? Something sweet. His father's hair was thick with oil.

Saul greeted Abner.

"What happened to you?" Abner demanded.

Saul's expression closed. "I've been looking for the donkeys."

Abner stepped closer. "You ate with Samuel!"

Saul lifted his shoulders and turned toward home. "When we saw the donkeys were not to be found, we went to him. Jehiel had a little money with him as a gift."

"And Samuel took it?" Abner seemed surprised.

"No," Jehiel was quick to say.

"Tell me what happened."

Saul glowered at Abner. "Samuel told me to go ahead to the high place."

Jonathan sensed the subtle change in his father's demeanor. Something momentous had happened, but he was unwilling to explain.

Abner put his hand on Saul. "What did Samuel say to you?"

Saul jerked free. "He assured us that the donkeys had been found." He stared hard at Abner. "And they have, haven't they?"

"Yes."

Without another word, Saul headed toward Gibeah.

Abner turned in frustration. "Jehiel!" He walked with the servant, speaking quietly. The man spread his hands and shrugged.

Jonathan caught up to his father and walked with him.

Saul gave a harsh laugh. "Jehiel knows nothing."

"Is there something to know, Father?"

Saul pressed his lips together.

Jonathan's heart thumped. "I smelled incense—"

Saul flashed him a look. Color surged into his face. "Say nothing of it to anyone. Do you understand?"

"Yes."

Jonathan said nothing more, but he was afraid Kish's prayers might have been answered.

✦   ✦   ✦

Saul refused to talk about his meeting with Samuel. He returned to work and plowed, while Kish and the others speculated on what had happened. Jonathan labored with his father, waiting for him to say something about what had happened in Naioth. But his father said nothing, working in silence, pensive and nervous. Jonathan refrained from pressing him like the others had.

But he spoke to his mother about it.

"Of course something happened," she whispered. "I'm afraid to think what it might have been. Just stay close to your father. Do whatever he asks of you. When he's ready, he'll probably tell you first before the others. I think he'll need you in the days ahead."

"Did he say anything to you?"

"No, but sometimes a man's silence speaks louder than his words."

Kish came out to the fields. "Let the servants do the rest of the plowing, my son. You are too important to do such work."

Saul glowered. "I'm a farmer, nothing more."

"Yes, we are farmers. But you may be called to something greater than that."

"I cannot live your dream, Father."

"We are summoned to Mizpah."

"Summoned?"

"Samuel has sent word that everyone is to gather at Mizpah."

Saul turned ashen. "Why?"

"Why do you think?" Kish was taut with excitement. "Samuel is going to tell us whom God has chosen to rule over Israel."

Saul put his hand to the plow. "Judah will rule."

"Judah?" Kish gave a derisive laugh. "There has not been a mighty man in Judah since Caleb and Othniel died. Judah!"

"It is the prophecy!" Saul didn't raise his head. "Jacob said—"

"And you think that gives Judah the right to rule over us? How many centuries ago was that?"

"Then *you* go! You're the head of our clan! Maybe we'll all get lucky and you'll be king! I'm staying here."

Kish's face reddened. "We *all* go! Samuel has summoned *all* the people. *All* of us! Do you understand?" He shook his head when Saul snapped the reins and bent his strength to the plow. "We leave tomorrow!" Kish shouted after him. He looked at Jonathan. "We leave at dawn!" He strode away.

Jonathan signaled a servant and left him in charge of

his team of oxen. He went after his father. Saul paused at the end of the field, and ran a shaking hand down over his face. Jonathan heard him mutter an angry prayer. Saul stood still, staring off into the distance. Jonathan stood near him, waiting, uncertain what to say. "What's wrong?"

Saul gave a bitter laugh. "Why should anything be wrong? Other than everyone is making plans for *my* life!" He gave Jonathan a stricken look. "A man should be able to say yes or no, shouldn't he?"

Jonathan didn't know what to say.

Saul shook his head and looked back over the newly plowed field. "He can't be right."

Was he talking about Kish? or someone else? "Whatever happens, Father, I'll stand with you."

Saul let out his breath slowly. "You won't have any choice." He handed Jonathan the reins and goad and walked slowly toward Gibeah, shoulders slumped.

+   +   +

All Israel gathered at Mizpah. Jonathan had never seen so many people in his life! Thousands upon thousands of tents had been erected, and the multitude pressed close, murmuring like the rumble of a storm ready to rain praises on the king God had chosen.

When Samuel came out, not a man, woman, or child spoke. Here and there, a baby cried, but was quickly soothed into silence.

"This is what the Lord, the God of Israel, has declared!" Samuel raised his arms.

Jonathan's heart pounded.

"I brought you from Egypt and rescued you from the

Egyptians and from all of the nations that were oppressing you. But though I have rescued you from your misery and distress, you have rejected your God today and have said, 'No, we want a king instead!' Now, therefore, present yourselves before the Lord by tribes and clans."

Samuel watched the clans of each tribe pass by him; the Levites, the Reubenites, the Simeonites and sons of Judah, then the tribe of Dan and Naphtali. The brush and scrape of sandals and bare feet were all that was heard, for no one dared utter a word as the prophet watched and waited for the Lord to tell him who would be king. The Gadites and Asherites, sons of Issachar and Zebulun passed him. Then the half-tribes of Manasseh and Ephraim descended from Joseph. Only the tribe of Benjamin remained.

Jonathan's stomach clenched tight. The closer they came to Samuel, the harder his heart pounded. His father wasn't beside him. He couldn't see his father anywhere. Where was he? He could feel the excitement in the air. Kish strode forward—head high, eyes bright, face flushed. Did he know Saul was missing?

"Benjamin!" Samuel called out, and Jonathan's heart leapt into his throat.

A rush of quiet voices rippled like water cascading over rock.

"Come forward clan by clan," Samuel told them.

The men of Benjamin obeyed.

Kish looked around. He grasped Jonathan's arm. "Where is your father?"

"I don't know."

"Matri!" Samuel called out.

Kish looked around again, his eyes frantic.

"Kish!" Samuel's voice rang out. "The Lord has appointed Saul king over Israel."

The tribe of Benjamin burst out in cheers and jumped up and down.

"Saul!" Kish turned this way and that. *"Saul!"*

The voices rose—some in triumph, some in question.

Jonathan looked around, searching. *Oh, Father. Father!* Where could he have gone?

Kish's face darkened. He grabbed one of his sons and beckoned the others. "Find your brother! Quickly! Go! Before these cheers turn to jeers! *Go!"*

"Has the man come here yet?" some called out.

Samuel looked grim. "Yes. He has hidden himself among the baggage."

Jonathan felt the blood drain from his face and then flood back until he felt on fire with embarrassment. He ducked his head and wove through the men.

Some began to shout. "Hiding? How can such a man save us?"

"What sort of champion will he be?"

Jonathan ran toward the piles of baggage, as eager to find his father as he was to escape disdain and contemptuous words. Hiding? Surely not! His father was no coward!

Jonathan found his father huddled among the bundles and sacks, shoulders slumped, head in his hands.

"You're the king, Father. The Lord has made you king!"

Saul groaned in misery. "Tell Samuel it's all a mistake."

"God told Samuel it's you. God doesn't make mistakes." Jonathan hunkered down beside him. "You must come." He fought tears, humiliation gathering. What if others saw his father like this? He couldn't bear it. "The Lord will help you. Surely the Lord will not abandon the one He's chosen, even if He abandons the rest of us."

Saul raised his head. When he held out his hand, Jonathan grasped it and helped him to his feet. He could feel his father shudder when someone cried out, "There he is!"

Men surged toward them. They surrounded Saul and Jonathan. Saul covered his fear and straightened. He was a head taller than every other man around him. Handsome and strongly built, he stood like a king among them. Saul was swept along like a leaf on a river until he stood before Samuel.

The prophet held out his hand. "This is the man the Lord has chosen as your king. No one in all Israel is like him!"

Jonathan saw men of Judah sneer and whisper among themselves. Thankfully, the vast majority shouted, "Long live the king!"

"Listen to the Word of the Lord!" Samuel called out to the mass. Saul stood beside the seer, facing the people. Samuel opened a scroll and read from it. Some stood still and listened. Many fidgeted. A few whispered among themselves. Samuel looked out over the people.

"The Lord said a day would come when we would ask for a king. He said to appoint a fellow Israelite; he may not be a foreigner." He faced Saul. "The king must not build up a large stable of horses for himself or send his people to Egypt to buy horses, for the Lord has told you, 'You must never return to Egypt.' The king must not take many wives for himself, because they will turn his heart away from the Lord. And he must not accumulate large amounts of wealth in silver and gold for himself."

Samuel took a smaller scroll and placed it upon the altar

he had made of stones, and then handed Saul the Torah. "Saul, son of Kish, son of Abiel, son of Zeror, son of Becorath, son of Aphiah of Benjamin, you must copy for yourself this body of instruction on a scroll in the presence of the Levitical priests. You must always keep that copy with you and read it daily as long as you live. That way you will learn to fear the Lord your God by obeying all the terms of these instructions and decrees. This regular reading will prevent you from becoming proud and acting as if you are above your fellow citizens. It will also prevent you from turning away from these commands in the smallest way. And it will ensure that you and your descendants will reign for many generations in Israel."

Saul took the scroll and held it at his side like a sword. Samuel turned him toward the people. Saul's jaw locked as he looked out over the thousands upon thousands staring at him. He looked but said nothing.

Jonathan was filled with pride as he observed his father. No one could say that he had coveted the power of kingship. Saul had all the eagerness of a man who had just received a sentence of death. But no man among all Israel looked more like a king than Saul, son of Kish.

Whatever it takes, Lord, help me to help my father, Jonathan prayed. *Give me strength when he needs protection. Give me wisdom when he needs counsel. Put mighty men around him, warriors who fear You and will faithfully serve the king.*

✦   ✦   ✦

Jonathan thought their lives would change, but as soon as the family reached Gibeah, his father turned to his field, leaving without orders those who returned with them and were eager to do the king's bidding. They built camps around the town and waited.

"Are you going to copy the Law, Father?"

"The fields must come first."

Troubled, Jonathan went to his mother. "The seer commanded it, Mother. Surely Samuel will be displeased if Father doesn't do it."

"Saul is king of Israel now, Jonathan, and every king does what is pleasing in his own sight. If your father won't copy the Law, there's nothing you can do about it. Do not waste time arguing with him. As strong as Kish is, has your grandfather ever won a battle with Saul?"

"No."

"Your father had no ambitions to be king, but whether he likes it or not, he is. And whether you want to be or not, you are the prince, heir to the throne."

His mother was shrewd. Everything she said meant something. "What are you saying, Mother? I would prefer you tell me outright."

She spread her hands. "Is it for a woman to tell a man what he should do?"

"All I want is to serve Father."

She folded her hands in her lap and smiled enigmatically. "Then serve him."

Ah. If the Law must be written and his father had no time to do it, then he must.

He went out into the field and asked permission to go to the school of prophets in Naioth. Saul nodded. "Finish the task as quickly as possible and come home." He embraced Jonathan, kissed him, and let him go.

By the time Jonathan returned to the house, his mother had already made preparations for his journey.

JONATHAN unrolled the scroll a little farther, secured it, and carefully dipped his stylus into the ink. He copied each letter, jot, and tittle exactly as it was written in the Law handed down by Moses. His lip was raw from chewing on it, the back of his neck ached, and his shoulder muscles were knotted; but he finished the line, set the stylus aside, and leaned back, wiping the sweat from his forehead.

"Enough for today."

Startled, Jonathan glanced up and saw Samuel watching him. The seer's face was solemn, his eyes glowing with inner fire. Jonathan never felt at ease when he looked into Samuel's face, this man who heard the voice of God and spoke His Word to the people.

As Jonathan stood, Samuel took the scroll, rolled it carefully, placed it inside its covering, and put it away.

"The letter of the Law is important, my prince, but you must also understand what it says."

Jonathan recited, "'Honor your father and mother. Then you will live a long, full life in the land the Lord your God is giving you.'" He saw the frown that crossed the seer's face and felt heat flood his own. Had Samuel thought him impertinent, or worse—disrespectful? Jonathan wished he had not said something that might be misconstrued as criticism of the prophets' sons, whose reputations were as different from Samuel's as the sun was from the earth. Jonathan swallowed hard, debating. If he apologized, he might have to explain.

"You walked all the way to this school of prophets to copy the Law. Why not one closer to home?"

"You were here, my lord."

Samuel's eyes darkened. "Do not call me lord." He pointed up. "There is only one Lord. The Lord God of Abraham, Isaac, and Jacob, the God of heaven and earth."

Jonathan hung his head. Better to say nothing than to cause more offense.

"Did your father the king send you here?"

How should he answer? He did not want the prophet to know that Saul thought the fields more important than the law of God.

"You won't answer?"

"He gave me permission to come."

"Why is your father not with you?"

Jonathan's heart thumped. "The king has matters of great importance—"

"More important than copying the Law?"

A rebuke! "No. I will give it to him."

Samuel shook his head. "Everyone heard what I said to your father at the coronation at Gilgal. You were standing right there beside him, weren't you?"

"Yes." Jonathan's palms sweated. Was God listening? "You said the king was to have a copy of the Law, read it every day, and carry it with him at all times."

"The *king* is to write a copy of the Law in his own hand."

Jonathan could not promise that his father would take the time to make his own copy. Despite the warriors who had followed Saul back to Gibeah, the king kept to his fields. Maybe he hoped they would grow tired of waiting and go home. But would God allow that to happen? It was one thing to want to be king, another entirely to be called by God to be king.

"Are you afraid to say anything?"

Jonathan looked up at the seer. "I don't know what my father is thinking. He is pressed from all sides. I didn't want to add to his burdens."

Samuel's expression gentled. He held out his hand. "Sit." He approached and sat on the bench with Jonathan. He rested his hands on his knees. "If you wish to honor and serve your father, tell him the truth. If you always speak the truth to the king, he will have reason to trust you, even when he doesn't like what you say."

"As the people trust you."

A flicker of pain crossed the seer's face. "If Saul obeys the Law, the Lord will give him victory over our enemies, and Israel *may* complete the work God gave them to do when they entered Canaan."

"My father will listen."

"It is not enough to listen, my son. One must obey."

Jonathan was certain his father would have come himself to copy the Law if he had not had so many other responsibilities. He worried about preparing the fields. He worried about the quality of the seed. He worried about sun and rain. He had always worried about many things. Now he had the entire nation to concern him. "Can any one man hold the future of Israel in his hands?"

Samuel shook his head. "God holds the future in His hands."

"May I ask you something?" Jonathan hoped Samuel would agree, for one thing had continued to plague him. He couldn't sleep for worrying about it.

Samuel inclined his head.

"You told us at Mizpah that we sinned by asking for a king. Has God forgiven us, Abba? or will His wrath be poured out upon my father? Saul did not ask to be king."

Samuel's gaze softened. "God calls whom He calls, Jonathan. The people have what they want: a king who stands tall among men. The Lord is compassionate upon His people. When we confessed before Him, He forgave us. God knows the hearts of men, my prince. He gave us commandments to follow so that we will not fall into sin. He knew Israel would one day ask for a king, and He told Moses what that king must be: a brother, a man who writes the Law in his own hand, studies it, is able to teach it, and abides by it all the days of his life."

When Jonathan returned home, he would tell his father everything Samuel said.

"You have great confidence in your father, don't you?"

"Yes!" Jonathan nodded. He was proud of his father. "I think I have more confidence in my father than he has in himself."

"He will learn what it means to be a king."

Who else could Jonathan trust but the prophet of God? "Now that he is king, he has enemies on every side. Some of the other tribes cried out against him when God made him king."

"There will always be men who stand against the one God calls to serve Him." Samuel turned and placed his right hand upon Jonathan's shoulder. "Honor your father, my son, but let your confidence be in the Lord our God. I know you love Saul, as well you should. But do not allow your love to blind you. Do not keep silent if you see your father, the king, sin. Learn the Law and counsel the king wisely. You are his eldest son, first show of his strength, and heir to his throne. Much will be expected of you. Seek wisdom from the Lord. Study the Law, and encourage your father to do the same. But do not ever think you can do the work for him. The king must know the Lord our God and the power of His strength."

Jonathan nodded again, accepting every word Samuel said as though it came from God Himself.

"I have watched you work, my son. You wash your hands before you enter the chamber and tremble when you open the scroll."

"To hold the Law is a wondrous thing, Abba, but to copy it is a terrifying task."

Samuel's eyes grew moist. He put his hands on his knees and pushed himself up. "I will look over your work."

"Thank you, Abba."

Samuel patted Jonathan's shoulder. "I wish all men revered the Law as you do."

Jonathan bowed his head, embarrassed. "I must confess I would rather be a student of the Law than a prince."

Samuel put his hand on Jonathan's head. "You can be both."

✦   ✦   ✦

Jonathan returned home with the copy of the Law carefully packed for travel. A small portion of it was tucked into a leather cylinder hidden beneath his tunic. He would keep it near his heart at all times.

How he looked forward to sitting with his father and discussing the Law, plumbing its meanings, relishing the richness of it. Each day that he had worked on making the copy, he had thought how wonderful it was going to be to share it with the king.

He found his father still in the fields, and warriors still encamped around Gibeah, waiting for the king to give them orders. Kish looked haggard. Jonathan overheard his low, heated words to Abner. "I dare say nothing to Saul that can be overheard or these men who wait upon him will think him more of a coward! What is my son waiting for?"

Jonathan was troubled by the talk. God had chosen his father as king. No one could doubt that! God would tell Saul when to act and what to do.

To pass the time, warriors sparred with one another. They trained for war daily while waiting for a command. Saul's habits did not change. He arose with the sun, yoked his oxen, and went out to work. When he returned, he ate with his family and guests.

Jonathan offered numerous times to read the Law to his father, but Saul always said, "Later. I'm tired."

Reaching for more bread, Kish spoke to his son in a quiet, hard whisper. "You must do something or these men will desert you! They will not wait forever for you to take the reins of kingship."

Tense lines appeared around Saul's eyes. "And everything you planned and sacrificed for will be lost. Isn't that right, Father?"

"I didn't do it for me." Kish spoke between his teeth. "I did it for you, for our family, for our people! Do you wait because you're angry with me?"

"No."

"Then what holds you back?"

"I will wait until I have some sign of what I am to do."

"Some sign?" Kish flung the bread down. Realizing others watched, he bared his teeth in a smile and leaned forward for some dates. When the others began to talk again, Kish glanced at Jonathan and then back to Saul. "A sign from whom? What sort of sign do you need other than the crown upon your head and these men who wait to obey your least command?"

Burned by his grandfather's sarcasm, Jonathan leaned over so that he could see past his father. "*God* will tell the king what to do and when to do it."

"A child's faith."

Heat surged into Jonathan's face.

Saul clenched his hand. "My son speaks more wisdom than anyone at this table!"

The room was silent.

Florid, Kish held his tongue. When Saul rose, Kish followed. Jonathan followed both men. "You have barely three thousand men," Kish stormed when they were out of hearing. "The rest refuse to follow a king who hides among the baggage!"

Saul turned, his face as red as his father's. "I felt unworthy to be king of Israel, but you got what you wanted, Father, didn't you?" He waved his hands in the air. "You and all my other ambitious relatives who thirst for Philistine blood!"

"God chose you."

"Convenient of you to remember that."

Jonathan stood, staring at them. It was not the first time he had seen them argue this way.

Kish lowered his voice. "Yes. We wanted one of our own to be king. Judah ruled for a time, but now it is time for the tribe of Benjamin to lead the nation to glory."

Benjamin, the youngest of Jacob's twelve sons. Benjamin, son of the beautiful Rachel, Jacob's favorite wife. Benjamin, Joseph's beloved baby brother. Though smallest among the twelve tribes, they were not least in arrogance!

"You must prove yourself worthy of respect, my son. You must punish those who refused to bring you gifts due a king. You must—"

"Must?" Saul glared, the cords in his neck standing out. "I wear the crown. Not you. God told Samuel to place it upon *my* head. Not yours. You have no right to command me to do anything anymore. Offer me advice when I ask for it, Father. If I ever ask. And never forget Jonathan is my heir."

Kish glanced back. Jonathan wondered if his grandfather realized he had been there the entire time. Muttering under his breath, Kish left them. Saul let out his breath and shook his head. "I need to be alone."

When his father left him, Jonathan found a quiet place and a lamp. He took his scroll from its casing and read. Someone cleared his throat softly. He turned.

A servant appeared from the shadows. "Your mother requests the pleasure of your company, my prince."

Rolling the scroll, he tucked it back into its case. His mother. She always knew every word that was spoken in the household.

When he entered his mother's quarters, she was working at her loom. Without looking up, she said, "Your father and grandfather had words." She turned to face him. "When the time comes, you will stand at your father's right hand and help him command his army."

Distracted, Jonathan watched his sisters.

His mother called to them. Merab came quickly, but Michal ignored them both.

"Get your sister out of the wool. It's yet to be carded. She already reeks." She glanced at him, frustrated. "I have so much to say to you."

Jonathan's brothers Malkishua and Abinadab clattered sticks as they sparred like the warriors outside the walls. Jonathan grinned. "Gibeah is alive with men eager to follow the king."

A servant brought his youngest brother, Ishbosheth, to his mother. The infant cried and sucked on his fist. "Saul is first among our people, Jonathan." His mother took the baby. "And you are second. You must be as wise as a serpent. Kish will come to you now with his advice. Listen to him and hold on to what will best serve your father, for that will serve you best as well." Ishbosheth screamed for what he wanted. "And may God grant us peace."

Jonathan left, relieved that whatever else his mother had to say would have to wait until later.

+   +   +

"Someone is coming!" the watchman called out. Jonathan ran to the gate of the city, where his grandfather and uncles had been holding court. Strangers appeared, stumbling with exhaustion, dust covered, faces streaming sweat. Jonathan pressed through the crowd to hear.

"We come from Jabesh-gilead . . ." The city, belonging to the tribe of Manasseh, lay east of the Jordan River, south of the Sea of Galilee in Manasseh's territory. ". . . to ask the king what we must do."

"Give our brothers water." Kish waved his hand. "Quickly, so they can tell us what's happened!"

Warriors gathered as the panting messengers grasped wooden cups and gulped water. "Nahash," one managed before draining another cup. People whispered among themselves: "The snake!" Everyone had heard of the Ammonite king and feared invasion. Refreshed, the messenger addressed Kish and the other city leaders. "Nahash has besieged us. The elders pleaded for a treaty with him, and promised to be his servants, but he said he will only agree if he gouges out the right eye of every man in the city as a disgrace to all Israel!"

If Nahash got his way, Jabesh-gilead would be defenseless for years to come, and an open doorway to the territory of the other tribes of Israel.

Men wailed and tore their clothing. "God has forsaken us!"

Women screamed and wept.

Jonathan saw his father returning with the oxen and ran out to meet him. Saul looked past him at the wailing mob. "What's the matter? Why is everyone crying?"

So they told him about the message from Jabesh. "The snake has laid siege to Jabesh-gilead." One of the messengers had told Saul everything by the time Abner and Kish came toward them.

Saul spread his arms wide and made a sound unlike anything Jonathan had ever heard from any man before. Terrified, he drew back from his father. The people stared and fell silent. Saul's roar made the hair on Jonathan's neck stand on end.

Face fiery red, eyes blazing, Saul threw the yoke off his oxen. He strode to a man who had been chopping wood and took his ax, then cried out as he raised it and brought it down on the lead ox. The animal dropped and jerked with death throes while Saul moved to the second and killed it as well. No one moved; no one uttered a sound as the king of Israel kept swinging that ax until he had dismembered his oxen.

Tunic soaked in blood, ax still in hand, Saul faced the people. Children ducked behind their mothers. Men drew back, even Kish, who stared, white-faced.

"Send out messengers!" King Saul buried his ax in the severed head of the lead ox. He pointed to the carcasses. "This is what will happen to the oxen of anyone who refuses to follow Saul and Samuel into battle! *We muster at Bezek*!"

Grinning, Abner turned and shouted eleven names, ordering them to spread the word. "And tell them a king rules in Israel!"

Jonathan still stared at his father, convinced he had heard the voice of God come out of him. "King Saul!" he shouted, raising his fists in the air. "King Saul!"

Every warrior raised his hands and shouted with him.

✦ ✦ ✦

Three hundred thousand Hebrews came to Bezek, thirty thousand more from the tribe of Judah. Even those who had turned their backs on Saul and mocked him now waited eagerly for his command! The prophet Samuel stood at Saul's right hand, Jonathan to his left.

Saul spoke to his officers. "Where are the messengers from Jabesh-gilead?"

The question was shouted. Men pressed forward, separating themselves from the throng of warriors. "Here, my lord!"

"Return to your city and say, 'We will rescue you by

noontime tomorrow!' Tell the elders to say to the Ammonites that the city will surrender and Nahash can do whatever seems best." He laughed coldly. The Ammonites did not know the king of Israel had mustered an army. "They will return to their camp and celebrate. It will be the last time, for at the last night watch, we attack!"

Men raised their spears and clubs and cheered. Jonathan grinned in pride. No one doubted his father was king now! Let the enemies of Israel see God's chosen in battle!

"Abner!" Saul beckoned.

"Yes, my lord!"

"Separate the men into three divisions. If one division is destroyed, there will be two others to continue fighting. If two fall, one will be left." Each commander knew the route he was to take.

Where did his father come by such knowledge and confidence? It could only come from the Lord God!

Samuel stretched out his arms before the fighting men. "May the God of our fathers go out before you!"

Jonathan stayed at his father's side as they marched by night the seventeen miles down the mountains and across the Jordan River. Fear tightened his belly, but he let no one know. When the army came near the Ammonite camp, all was quiet, the guards asleep at their posts.

"Now!" Saul commanded. Jonathan and several others raised the rams' horns and blew. Israel's war cry rose to the heavens.

Saul held his sword high. There were only two in all Israel. Jonathan drew the other and raised it. Shouting, the thousands ran full out toward the Ammonite camp where confusion reigned.

When three Ammonites rose up to attack his father,

rage fired Jonathan's blood. He cut down one and sliced through another. His father killed the third. Excitement flooded Jonathan's blood.

Jonathan's strength held all morning as he protected his father. Any man who dared try to reach the king of Israel died. By the time the sun was overhead, Nahash and his army lay slaughtered upon the field. Screams from the dying were silenced. The few who survived had scattered before the scourging fire of the Lord.

Thrusting his bloody sword into the air, Jonathan shouted in victory. *"For the Lord and Saul!"*

Others joined in his ecstatic praise.

But the bloodlust of killing Ammonites darkened and turned on those who had mocked Saul the day Samuel declared him king. The Benjaminites shouted, "Now where are those men who said, 'Why should Saul rule over us?' Bring them here, and we will kill them!"

Men who had fought side by side against the Ammonites now turned on one another, voices raised.

Jonathan remembered the Law he had written. "Father!" He had to shout to be heard. "We are brothers, sons of Jacob!"

Saul pulled him back from the fray and cried out, "No one will be executed today!" The throng quieted. Saul looked at Kish and the others and raised his voice for all to hear. "For today *the Lord has rescued Israel*!"

Samuel raised his staff. "Come, let us all go to Gilgal to renew the kingdom."

"To Gilgal!" men shouted. "To Gilgal!"

Jonathan's heart beat with a fear deeper than what he had felt in battle against the Ammonites. These men who

turned so swiftly against one another might just as quickly
turn against his father. He stayed close to Saul.

The throng of fighting men moved like a giant flock
across the hillsides. For years, they had bunched together
in small pockets of discontent, bleating in fear and uncer-
tainty, ignoring the voice of the Shepherd, and looking
about for one of their own to lead the way. Now, they followed Saul.

Saul had proven himself today, but Jonathan knew his
father would have to continue to prove himself over and
over again or these men would scatter once more.

God's people were like sheep, but today Jonathan had
seen how quickly they could turn into wolves.

+   +   +

Gilgal! Jonathan drank in the sight, remembering the history he had written and now wore around his neck. The
children of Israel had crossed the Jordan River and
entered the Promised Land here. It was on this plain they
had first camped and then renewed their covenant with
God. It was here the Angel of the Lord had appeared to
Joshua and given him the battle plan to take Jericho, the
gateway to Canaan.

What better place for his father to be reaffirmed king of
Israel! After years of every man living in fear and doing
what was right in his own eyes, God had given them a
king to unite them!

May You instruct Saul and bless all Israel, O Lord!

Samuel stood at the monument of twelve stones the
tribes had brought from the River Jordan to commemorate
their crossing over. A sea of warriors stood silent as the

old prophet—bent in frame, but still quick in mind and the Spirit of the Lord—spoke.

"I have done as you asked and given you a king. Your king is now your leader. I stand here before you—an old, gray-haired man—and my sons serve you."

Despised by all.

"Here I stand!" Samuel held his arms outstretched. "I have served as your leader from the time I was a boy to this very day. Now testify against me in the presence of the Lord and before His anointed one. Whose ox or donkey have I stolen? Have I ever cheated any of you? Have I ever oppressed you? Have I ever taken a bribe and perverted justice? Tell me and I will make right whatever I have done wrong."

Jonathan felt tears well at the pain in Samuel's voice. All because his sons had brought shame upon his house. *Lord, let me never bring shame upon my father! Let my actions be honorable.*

He stepped forward, unable to bear the pain he saw in Samuel's face. "You have not cheated us, Abba." His voice broke.

Samuel looked at Jonathan.

The people spoke, calling out here and there. "No! You have never cheated or oppressed us, and you have never taken even a single bribe."

Tears streamed down Samuel's cheeks. He turned to Saul. "The Lord and His anointed one are my witnesses today, that my hands are clean." His voice was harsh with pent-up emotion.

"I am witness." Saul bowed his head in respect.

"He is witness! The king is witness!"

"God is witness!" Jonathan cried out.

Samuel's voice steadied when he spoke of Moses and
Aaron and the forefathers of all present who had come out
of Egypt. His voice filled with sorrow when he spoke of
their sins in serving the baals and ashtoreths of the
Canaanites rather than the Lord their God who had performed signs and wonders and delivered them from Egypt.
The people had forgotten the Lord! And the Lord gave
them into the hands of their enemies! Over the years,
when they cried out and repented, the Lord sent deliver-
ers—Gideon and Barak, Jephthah and Samson—to rescue
them from the hands of evildoers.

"But when you were afraid of Nahash, the king of
Ammon, you came to me and said that you wanted a king
to reign over you, even though the Lord your God was
already your king."

Jonathan hung his head. Had he once given thought to
what it meant for God to withdraw from His people so that
men could rule themselves? *He calls us His children and we
have rejected Him.* Jonathan's throat closed tightly. *Lord!
Let me never forget that You are my king.*

Samuel pointed. "All right, here is the king you have
chosen. You asked for him, and the Lord has granted your
request!"

Jonathan looked up at his father. Saul stood, head high,
and looked out over the tribes of Israel. He was no longer
the frightened man who had hidden in the baggage. His
face was fierce, challenging. The Law felt heavy against
Jonathan's chest.

"Now if you fear and worship the Lord and listen to His
voice, and if you do not rebel against the Lord's commands, then both you and your king will show that you
recognize the Lord as your God. But if you rebel against

the Lord's commands and refuse to listen to Him, then *His hand will be as heavy upon you as it was upon your ancestors!*"

Jonathan put his hand over his heart, feeling the Law encased there. *Mercy, Lord. Have mercy upon us!*

"Now—" Samuel's voice deepened—"stand here and see the great thing the Lord is about to do. You know that it does not rain at this time of the year during the wheat harvest. I will ask the Lord to send thunder and rain today. Then you will realize how wicked you have been in asking the Lord for a king!"

People murmured and shifted nervously. If God sent rain now, the crops would be ruined. Jonathan studied the sky. Clouds were forming; already the sky was darkening.

Saul groaned.

Jonathan knew all his father's hard work would gain him nothing. He shut his eyes. *Lord, we have sinned! I love my father, but we have all done an evil thing in asking for a king. Forgive us.*

Jonathan's heart quickened as clouds swirled. Lightning flashed, followed by a deep rumble that pressed upon him. And then the rain came, cold against victory-heated pride.

Jonathan bowed his head. *You are God! You are the God of Ahimaaz. You are my God and there is no other!*

Saul wailed. "The wheat is ready for harvest. The stalks will get wet. The grain will rot."

Jonathan raised his head and smiled at his father. "The Lord will provide."

Samuel turned and looked at Jonathan, and the sorrow slowly ebbed from his eyes.

Jonathan raised his hands, palms up and felt the drops

of rain hit against him—sharp, cold spears. "Wash us, Lord. Cleanse us of sin." *You are king!*

Men screamed. "Samuel! Pray to the Lord your God for us, or we will die! For now we have added to our sins by asking for a king."

Jonathan prayed. "Without You, we can do nothing for Your people. Command us, Lord. Let it be as it once was. Go out before us and stand at our backs."

Lightning flashed again. Jonathan shuddered and dropped to his knees. He bowed his face to the ground, rain drenching him. "Lord, forgive us."

"Don't be afraid!" Samuel called out in a loud voice. "You have certainly done wrong, but make sure now that you worship the Lord with all your heart, and don't turn your back on Him. Don't go back to worshiping worthless idols that cannot help or rescue you—they are totally useless! The Lord will not abandon His people, because that would dishonor His great name. For it has pleased the Lord to make you His very own people."

Jonathan wept. He met Samuel's gaze, filled with compassion and tenderness.

"As for me—" Samuel spread his hands and looked at Saul and then at the multitude—"I will certainly not sin against the Lord by ending my prayers for you. And I will continue to teach you what is good and right. But be sure to fear the Lord and faithfully serve Him. Think of all the wonderful things He has done for you!"

Jonathan came to his feet, remembering all he had copied. God had delivered them from Egypt, given them land to till and plant, children. *You created us, Lord. You gave us life and breath.*

The rain softened, refreshingly cool against his face.

Samuel gazed out over the nation. "But if you continue to sin, you and your king will be swept away."

I am Saul's son, Lord, but I want to be Your man. I want a heart like Samuel's. Undivided. Devoted to You. Lord, Lord, make it so.

✦ ✦ ✦

Saul chose three thousand of the best warriors and sent the rest of the army home. Jonathan wondered why. "Aren't we going to attack the Philistine outposts?"

"I have no quarrel with the Philistines."

No quarrel? "But Father, they've oppressed us for years."

"We have two swords between us and no blacksmiths. That's reason enough not to start a war with them."

Had his father so quickly forgotten the lesson of Jabesh-gilead? "God is our strength!"

"Winning one battle against the Ammonites does not mean we can win a war against the Philistines."

"But the Lord gave us victory over Nahash. We need not return home, tails tucked between our knees."

Abner grasped Jonathan's shoulder, fingers biting in warning. "We will discuss all this as we travel south."

The army camped at Micmash. The king had no plans to attack the Philistine outpost at Geba, even though it was close enough to threaten Gibeah. Jonathan listened at the military counsel meetings, but heard nothing that would solve the threat to his father's reign if the warriors at Geba moved against Gibeah.

So he spoke again. "It is not wise to have enemies so close to our home. Saul is king of Israel, and Gibeah is now center of the nation. What is to stop the Philistines from attacking my father?"

Saul looked at Abner and then at the others for an answer. When they gave none, he shrugged. "I will remain here in Micmash until we see how the Philistines take the news of Nahash's defeat."

What had happened to his father's boldness? Where was the fierce King Saul who had hacked two oxen to pieces and led Israel into battle? "What of Mother? What of your sons and daughters? Gibeah—"

Saul scowled. "You can go there and secure the city. Close the gates and guard the city."

Jonathan blushed. "I can't hide behind the city walls while you're here. My place is beside you against the enemies of God."

"You will go to Gibeah. I have Abner and three thousand of Israel's best to guard me. I'll stay here in Micmash as we plan for the days ahead. You go on home."

Didn't he understand? "The Ammonites are in fear of us. And the Philistines will be as well!"

Kish snorted. "Young blood flows hot with foolishness."

Saul glared at his father and then looked at Jonathan again. "Samuel is no longer with us."

"God is with us," Jonathan said.

"God was with me at Jabesh-gilead, but I do not feel His Presence with me now."

"Father—"

Saul's eyes darkened. "The Philistines are not the cowards the Ammonites are."

Jonathan moved closer and lowered his voice so the

others wouldn't hear. "If the Ammonites were cowards, Father, why did we fear them so long?"

Saul's head came up, eyes flashing; but Jonathan knew the fear that lurked behind the king's quick temper.

Kish smiled and patted Jonathan on the back. "There is a time for everything, Jonathan."

Lord, make them see! "Yes, but the time is now. Nahash is dead! The Ammonites are scattered. The Philistines will have heard how King Saul mustered the army and slaughtered the invaders. They were in fear of us before, my king, and they will be again. God is on our side! We have the advantage!"

Abner put his hand on Jonathan's shoulder. Jonathan shook it off.

Saul's eyes glowed. "No one doubts your courage, my son."

Kish's eyes flickered. "But courage must be tempered with wisdom."

Jonathan looked at his grandfather. "I thought you wanted war." He looked around at the others. "Do not dismiss what I say."

"There is a difference between the Ammonites who attempted to take land—" Saul waved his hand over the maps—"and the Philistines who have occupied it for years. They have strongholds."

"It is our land, Father, the land God gave us. It's time we drove them back into the sea from which they came!"

Saul raised his hands. "Using what against them? They have iron weapons. We have two swords. Our warriors carry dull mattoxes, ruined axes, chipped sickles and spears. Even if we had a blacksmith, do I have the shekels to pay to sharpen weapons for an army? And if I did, the

Philistines would know we were preparing for war, and they'd come down on us and drown us in our own blood."

"So we wait? We do nothing when they raid our crops?"

"What crops?" Kish ground out. "God destroyed the wheat."

"We wait, my son. We plan."

Fear still reigned in Israel!

Jonathan's father put his arm around him and walked him to the entrance of the tent. "You go to Gibeah with the men I've assigned you. Secure the city."

Jonathan bowed his head and left the tent. He would go to Gibeah and do exactly what his father commanded.

And then he would destroy Geba before the Philistines there had time to attack and destroy his father!

✦   ✦   ✦

Raging, Saul paced before Jonathan, who was still exultant over the defeat of Geba. "What sort of message does it give all Israel when my own son doesn't listen to me?"

"I secured Gibeah."

"And destroyed Geba! You have brought disaster on us all! Did you think killing a few hundred Philistines and burning a small outpost would accomplish anything? You pulled the tail of a lion and now he will turn and devour us! When word spreads of what you did, we will have all Philistia thirsting for our blood! *We are not ready for this war!*"

Jonathan shrank inwardly as doubt squelched his assurance that God had wanted him to attack the outpost. *Was I listening to my own pride?* If they obeyed God, would the Lord not give them victory on every side?

Would the Lord not help them rid their land of the Philistines just as He had helped them crush the Ammonites at Jabesh-gilead? "Samuel said—"

"Be silent! I am the king. Let me think . . ." Saul gripped his head. "I didn't expect rebellion from you!"

Abner cleared his throat. "My lord, what order shall I give the men?"

Saul lowered his hands and stared off into space.

"My lord?"

Saul turned, jaw set. "Send out messengers and have them blow the trumpets. Tell everyone I attacked the Philistine outpost." He glared at Jonathan. "Better if the people think *I* acted boldly than have them know my son acted in haste and without the backing of the king."

Humiliated, his confidence shredded by doubt, Jonathan said nothing.

✦   ✦   ✦

Jonathan went cold when he heard three thousand Philistine chariots had been sighted. Each bore a driver and a skilled warrior equipped with bow and arrows and several spears.

Saul paled. "How many soldiers?"

"Too many to count, my lord. They are as numerous as the grains of sand upon the seashore, and they're already at Beth-aven."

Worse news came the following morning. Some of Saul's warriors had deserted in the night. Terrified by the power of Philistia, others clustered and whispered among themselves. The men of Israel took to caves and thickets, hid among rocks and in pits and dry cisterns.

Saul returned to Gilgal and waited for Samuel. Jonathan

went with him, as did a young armor bearer Saul pressed
into Jonathan's service. What Ebenezer lacked in size, he
made up for in zeal.

Kish, Abner, and the others were full of advice for the
king, but the king listened to no one.

Racked with guilt, Jonathan spent hours in unceasing
prayer, asking for the Lord's forgiveness and pleading for
guidance. Though many cheered the victory at Geba, most
were sick with fear and ready to run.

Abner grew frustrated and confronted the king. "We
have less than two thousand warriors right now, my lord,
and more are deserting every day. You must make a decision."

Jonathan was afraid to give advice. He was afraid to
make claims about what God would do. No one could
question God's power, but every man alive in Israel ques-
tioned whether He would use it for their defense. Worse,
Jonathan realized now that his one small victory could
precipitate an all-out war. He looked out over the tents
and couldn't help wonder how so few could stand against
so many. Rather than rallying his father and his army,
Jonathan had succeeded only in bringing their fear to the
surface and sending thousands into hiding.

*What a sight we are! Lord, why is it so hard for Your peo-
ple to trust You when You've proven Your power and faithfulness to us time after time? Is it because we know we
continue to sin? How do we root out the sin in us? Our forefathers didn't listen to You, and now we don't. Only a few
days ago, You sent lightning and thunder and rain, and all
these men can think about is the ruined crops and what they
will eat when winter comes! You are God! You hold our lives
in the palms of Your hands!*

Fear spread like tares in the wheat until even Jonathan felt the roots of it sinking into his heart. Some of those who had been with him at Geba deserted. Each morning revealed more empty spaces among the camps of Saul's "best of Israel."

The king grew more and more frustrated. "The entire army will scatter before that old man gets here!"

Jonathan shuddered. *That old man?* Samuel was God's prophet, God's voice to the people. "He will come."

"Where is he? Why does he delay? He said he would come in seven days."

"It hasn't been seven days yet, Father."

"Soon, my entire army will have melted away."

Abner did what he could to rally the remaining warriors, but confidence in the king was at its lowest ebb and the prophet's warning was fresh in their minds. Their king had brought touble upon them. Forgotten was the victory over the Ammonites. All men could think of was the gathering storm of war, the three thousand chariots and multitude of foot soldiers getting ready to destroy them.

Jonathan felt he had to do something to make up for bringing all this on his father. *But what? What, Lord?* No answer came.

Jonathan awakened Ebenezer before dawn on the seventh day. "If my father misses me, tell him I've gone out to wait for Samuel." Jonathan went to the edge of the shrinking camp. Men huddled over their fires, ducking their heads when he glanced their way. He didn't want to think about what they might be discussing.

Because of me, Lord, they've lost hope in Your king.

The sun rose. There was no sign of Samuel. Jonathan worried. Had his actions at Geba caused the prophet trouble as well? What if the Philistines had taken him captive? Or worse, what if they had killed the aged man of God? He broke out in a cold sweat even thinking such thoughts.

Lord, we need him. He speaks Your Word to us. Please protect him and bring him to us. Oh, God, help us. Tell us what You want us to do! I thought I was stepping out in faith, but maybe my father and his advisors are right and I acted the fool. If so, forgive me, Lord. Let the trouble fall on my head and not my father's. Not on these men who shake with fear. Don't abandon us on my account, Lord.

Jonathan's armor bearer, Ebenezer, came running. "The king—" he rasped for breath—"the king wants you with him. He's going to make the sacrifice."

"What?" Jonathan ran as fast as he could, Ebenezer close behind him. When he reached his father's tent, he entered and went cold at the sight of the king wearing a priestly ephod. "No!" His lungs burned. His heart pounded so hard, he thought he would choke. He grasped the Law he wore around his neck. "You can't do this, Father. The Law says only a priest—"

"There is no priest!"

Terrified for all their sakes, Jonathan went to his father. "It's not midday yet, my lord. Samuel *will* come."

Sweat beaded on Saul's brow. "I called for him and he did not come. I can't wait any longer." His face was pale and strained.

"The Lord will not help us if you do this."

"My army! My men are leaving me! What would you have me do?" He looked around at all his advisors.

"Whatever is in your heart to do, my king." They all seemed to agree.

Jonathan looked from Abner to Kish to the others and

back to his father. "Samuel will come!" He stepped in front of his father. "Gideon had fewer men than we have, and he defeated the Midianites."

"I am not Gideon!"

"You were a farmer like him. The Spirit of the Lord came upon you, too. You gathered a force of three hundred and thirty thousand warriors and defeated the Ammonites!"

"And where are all my warriors now?" Saul yanked the flap of the tent aside. "Gone!"

"You have more than Gideon had. Nahash and the Ammonites are destroyed!"

"The Philistines are a worse scourge than the Midiantes or the Ammonites." Saul let the flap fall. He groaned, rubbing his eyes. "I never asked to be king. I never asked for any of this!"

"God chose you, Father." Jonathan spoke as calmly as he could, though their fear seeped into him. "Trust in the Lord and in the power of His strength!"

"And what does that mean?" Abner stepped forward. "In practical, tactical terms, Jonathan?"

"God could send lightning bolts on our enemies," Kish agreed. "Why doesn't He?"

Saul turned abruptly. "Where is the Ark?" They all looked at him. "Maybe if I had the Ark with me. The Philistines were afraid of it once. Remember?"

Jonathan felt a knot growing in his stomach. Did his father mean to use the Ark like an idol? "They captured the Ark."

"Yes. And a plague of mice and rats destroyed their crops. The Philistines were sick with tumors. Eventually they sent it back on a cart loaded down with gold." Saul

looked at Abner. "How long would it take to bring it
here?"

A warrior entered the tent. "There is still no sign of
Samuel, my lord."

Abner frowned. "There is no time. You must do something now before all the men are gone." Everyone agreed.

"Don't." Jonathan was a lone voice in the tent. He
looked into his father's face. "Wait. Please. Give the seer
more time."

Abner shook his head. "You know too little of men,
Jonathan. If we wait much longer, the camp will be empty
and the king will stand alone. How long do you think
your father will survive with just those of us inside this
tent to defend him?"

Abner's words swayed Saul. "Bring me the burnt offerings and the peace offerings. We can't ask God to help us
unless we give *Him* something."

Jonathan's heart pounded heavily, the pit of his stomach like a hard, cold ball of fear. He drew out the Law.
"You mustn't do this, Father. Please, listen. I can show
you—"

"Do you not yet understand?" Saul shouted. "I can't
wait." His eyes blazed. "I won't wait! Samuel promised he
would come. He didn't keep his word!" Saul went outside.
"Gather some stones. We'll build the altar right here." He
grabbed Jonathan's arm. "You will stand over there. And
say no more!" His chin jerked up. "The kings of other
nations make sacrifices before their armies. Why shouldn't
I?" Saul turned to Abner. "Call the men. They must see
what I do. Tell them I am making an offering to the Lord
so He will help us."

Jonathan turned to Ebenezer and spoke quietly.

"Station yourself where you can see anyone approaching camp. When you see Samuel, run back here like the wind and shout his coming. Hurry!"

"Yes, my lord." The boy drew back from the others, turned, and ran to do Jonathan's bidding.

As the young prince watched his father, he wondered if God would take Saul's fear into account. *Lord, forgive him. He doesn't know what he's doing.*

The men gathering looked pleased by what was about to happen. Had his father read, written, and studied the Law, he would know better than to defy the Lord like this! And those who followed him would know better than to trust their lives to the plans of men.

The sun hovered above the western horizon. A crippled calf was brought to Saul. Why kill a healthy one without blemish as the Law commanded? It seemed that as long as his father had decided to disregard one part of the Law, none of its other instructions mattered either. Jonathan watched as King Saul put his hands on the animal's head, prayed loudly for God's help, and then slit the calf's throat. Jonathan closed his eyes, sickened by the ceremony. Soon he smelled smoke, mingled with the stench of disobedience.

Dismissed, the men went about their duties. Saul looked at Jonathan and smiled, confident again. He went back inside his tent to talk with his advisors.

Jonathan sat, head in his hands.

Ebenezer came running. Face flushed, out of breath, he rasped, "The prophet comes."

Shame filled Jonathan. How could he face Samuel?

Saul came outside. "Come! We will meet him together!"

He spread his arms wide and smiled warmly. "Welcome, Samuel!"

Samuel's eyes blazed. His fingers whitened on his staff. "Saul! What is this you have done?"

Surprised, Saul frowned. He looked from the prophet to the men around him. "I saw my men scattering from me—" his eyes narrowed coldly—"and you didn't arrive when you said you would, and the Philistines are at Micmash ready for battle. So I said, 'The Philistines are ready to march against us at Gilgal, and I haven't even asked for the Lord's help!' So I felt compelled—" he swept his hand, taking in his advisors—"to offer the burnt offering myself before you came."

Jonathan looked between the two men. Wasn't his father's sin bad enough without trying to cast blame on the seer?

Samuel's glance took in everyone. "Leave us!"

Jonathan wanted to flee before the wrath that was sure to come.

"My son stays." Saul commanded Jonathan with a gesture.

Jonathan took his place beside his father. He could not desert him now: how could he when Geba had started all this?

Samuel stared at Saul. "How foolish! You have not kept the command the Lord your God gave you. Had you kept it, the Lord would have established your kingdom over Israel forever. But now your kingdom must end, for the Lord has sought out a man after His own heart. The Lord has already appointed him to be the leader of His people, because you have not kept the Lord's command."

Jonathan cringed.

Saul gritted his teeth in anger, but when the prophet turned away, the king took a step toward him. "You turn your back on me, Samuel? You turn your back on Israel's king? Where are you going?"

"I am going to Gibeah." Samuel sounded weary and disheartened. "I would advise you to do the same."

Saul kicked the dust. "Go and tell Abner to count the men we have left."

Tears pricked Jonathan's eyes as he watched the old prophet walk away. "We should follow Samuel, Father."

"After we find out how many men we have left."

Jonathan wanted to cry out in grief. What did it matter how many men stood with a king rejected by God? "Let me speak to him on your behalf."

"Go, if you think you can do any good." Saul turned away.

✦   ✦   ✦

Jonathan ran after Samuel.

Samuel turned when he came near and spoke to those accompanying him. They moved away. Samuel leaned heavily on his staff, his face etched with exhaustion and sorrow.

Jonathan fell to his knees and bowed his face to the ground.

"Stand up!"

Jonathan surged to his feet, trembling.

"Why do you chase after me? Do you mean to use your sword against me?"

"No!" Jonathan blanched. "My father means you no harm, nor do I! Please . . . I came to ask you to forgive me. The blame is mine!"

Samuel shook his head. "You did not perform the sacrifice."

Tears blurred Jonathan's eyes. "My father was afraid. Because of what I did at Geba, all this . . ." He could not see Samuel's expression or guess at what the seer thought. "I'm the one who attacked Geba and brought the Philistines' wrath upon us. When we heard of the forces that are coming against us, the men began to desert. My father—"

"Each man makes his decisions, Jonathan, and each bears the consequences of what he decides."

"But are we not also prey to circumstances around us?"

"You know better."

"Can there be no allowances for mistakes? for fear?"

"Who is the enemy, Jonathan?"

"The Philistines." Jonathan wept. "I don't want God to be our enemy. What can I do to make things right?"

Samuel put his hand on Jonathan's shoulder. "What do you wear against your heart, my son?"

Jonathan put his hand against his breastplate. "The Law."

"Did you write it in your own hand because you thought you would be king someday?"

Jonathan blinked. Had he? Samuel said that Saul's kingdom would not last now. Did that mean Israel would fall? Did that mean the people would all suffer at the hands of their enemies?

"You say nothing."

Jonathan searched his eyes. "I want to say no." He swallowed hard. "But do I know myself well enough to answer?"

"Speak the truth to the king no matter what the others

around him say. And pray for him, my son." Samuel
released him.

Jonathan longed for reassurance. "Will you pray for my
father?" Surely the prayers of a righteous man would be
heard by God.

"Yes."

Jonathan grasped hope. "Then the Lord our God will
not abandon us completely."

"God does not abandon men, my son. Men abandon
God." As the old prophet headed toward Gibeah, his com-
panions joined him.

Jonathan stood watching for a long time, praying for
Samuel's safety and for his father, the king, to repent.

✦   ✦   ✦

Samuel waited in Gibeah while the Philistines encamped
at Micmash. King Saul returned to Gibeah and held court
under the shade of a tamarisk tree. When no Israelite army
came out to meet the Philistines, the Philistines sent out
raiding parties. Ophrah was attacked, then Beth-horon.
Soon after, they plundered the borderland overlooking the
valley of Zeboim facing the desert.

Samuel returned to Ramah. Saul waited for a sign from
God or a word of encouragement from the prophet. None
came. He grew more sullen with each passing day. His
army of six hundred sank into despair. Abner and the
other leaders gave advice, but Saul didn't listen. Numerous plans were laid out and then rejected. The king
seemed incapable of action. Worse, he became suspicious.
"Send someone to keep watch over Samuel. If he goes anywhere, follow him and report back to me!"

"Samuel prays for you, Father."

"So you say, but can I trust him? He said God will choose another."

Reports came in that the Philistines were on the move again.

Jonathan heard all the talk and kept his eyes open. The inactivity wore on him as much as it did the others. Was this what war was like? Long weeks, sometimes months, of waiting? And then the terror and exhilaration of battle?

The Philistines took cruel delight in raiding when and where they pleased, for King Saul sent no one to stop them. Jonathan's father could not get his mind off Samuel's prophecy.

Something had to be done to rouse the king and the men of Israel, something to bring them together as they had been when the Lord gave them Jabesh-gilead!

Jonathan prayed, *Lord, help me. I don't want to make the same mistake I did with Geba!*

If Jonathan did anything, he must do it alone so the blame would fall only on him if he failed.

A Philistine detachment was camped at the pass at Micmash. Jonathan knew the area well. The slippery, thorny cliffs of Bozez and Seneh faced each other. But there was one place above, barely a furrow of land, where one man could hold ground and kill a score of Philistines, possibly more.

Jonathan might die. So be it. Better to die in battle with honor than live in fear of idol worshipers. He rose, shouldered the quiver of arrows, took up his bow, and left the city.

Ebenezer grabbed Jonathan's shield and his own bow and arrows and ran after him. "Where are we going, my lord?"

"To see what the Lord will do."

The boy stayed at his side, but Jonathan wondered if he would be brave enough to follow all the way.

When they were away from Gibeah, Jonathan faced Ebenezer. "Let's go across to the outpost of those pagans. Perhaps the Lord will help us, for nothing can hinder the Lord. He can win a battle whether He has many warriors or only a few!"

Ebenezer's eyes brightened. He grinned broadly. "Do what you think is best. I'm with you completely, whatever you decide."

Jonathan laughed. What would the Philistines make of the two of them?

When they reached the cliff opposite the Philistine encampment, Jonathan surveyed the gap between them and the enemy camp. *Lord, send me a sign that You will give those men into our hands!*

He felt a quickening, a flush of heat rushing through his veins, a *yes, go* rush of confidence. Jonathan pointed. "All right then. We will cross over and let them see us. If they say to us, 'Stay where you are or we'll kill you,' then we will stop and not go up to them. But if they say, 'Come on up and fight,' then we will go up. That will be the Lord's sign that He will help us defeat them."

Either way, they would fight against God's enemies. One way would bring certain death. The other victory.

Ebenezer nodded. "We can hold them off as long as we have arrows, my lord. And then you have your sword!"

Jonathan gripped the boy's shoulder. Whether in the gap or on the cliffs, the boy was as willing to die fighting as he was. Jonathan descended first, setting the pace.

Slipping once, he caught hold and regained his footing. "Watch it there, my friend. Move to your right. That's it."

When they had both reached the bottom, Jonathan moved out of the shadows into the open. He planted his feet and lifted his head. Ebenezer joined him.

"Look!" A man laughed from above. "The Hebrews are crawling out of their holes!" Other Philistines joined the watchman. A few warriors peered over the edge of the cliff. One spit. Their laughter echoed between the walls of the cliffs.

Jonathan's heart beat hard for battle. *Lord, please give them into our hands! Let them know there is a God in Israel!*

And the sign came.

"Come on up here, and we'll teach you a lesson!"

"Come on, climb right behind me, for the Lord will help us defeat them!" Jonathan ran at the cliff and started to climb, Ebenezer right behind him. Grasping hold of thick-rooted thornbushes, Jonathan pulled himself up. He found footholds and climbed like a lizard on a fortress wall, trailed by his young armor bearer.

Still laughing, the Philistine warriors moved back from the edge of the cliff. Jonathan could hear them. When he reached the top, he walked forward and took his stand. He grinned at the surprise on the Philistines' faces.

"A couple of boys!"

One of the Philistines drew his sword. "Both about to die!"

Ebenezer took his place near Jonathan.

One of the Philistines guffawed.

In one fluid motion, Jonathan shrugged the bow from his shoulder, whipped an arrow out, set it, and sent it straight and true to its target. The laughing Philistine fell back, an arrow between his eyes. Stunned, the others stared at Jonathan and then let out a battle roar, drew swords, and came at Jonathan and Ebenezer, who shot one arrow after another, and one after another, Philistines fell—twenty in all.

The shouting had roused the others. More shouting came from behind.

With his last arrow released, Jonathan drew his sword and gave his battle cry. *"For the Lord!"* The ground shook as Philistine warriors panicked and ran. Jonathan ran into the confusion and hacked down an officer. Ebenezer grabbed a spear and threw it into a fleeing Philistine. More screams rent the air.

"The shofar blows!" Ebenezer cried out. "The king is coming!"

Jonathan shouted in exultation. Israel was on the move! Philistines ran in terror. Jonathan spotted a few Hebrews among the Philistines. Whether they were men who had gone up to fight with the enemy or were captives did not matter now. "Fight for Israel or die!" Jonathan shouted, and the men turned as one and fought for Jonathan.

"The Ark!" Ebenezer shouted.

Jonathan looked back and saw the Ark. *No!* With a roar, he turned, enraged at the thought of the enemy getting their hands on it again. He ran into the Philistine camp, sword flashing. *No one will ever take the Ark from us!* He cut to the left. *No one will open it and desecrate it!* He cut to the right. *No one will take the Law from us!* He slashed and stabbed. *No one will open the jar and spill out the manna!* He sliced off a warrior's arm and cut off his head. *No one will break the staff of Aaron that sprouted leaves, bloomed, and bore almonds in a day!*

Jonathan screamed in rage as he fought. "*Jehovah-Roi! El Shaddai! Adonai!*" God our King! God Almighty! Lord!

And Philistines ran from him in terror.

From all directions, the Hebrews came. The king's army of six hundred swelled and advanced north from Gibeah. Men of Ephraim pressed in from the south.

Confusion reigned among the Philistines. Some fled toward Aijalon, others to Ophrah, trying to reach Beth-aven, their stronghold, the house of wickedness.

Taking up a spear, Jonathan kept after the Philistines, encouraging the other Israelites who had joined him. They grew weary and faint, and were barely able to keep up with him. When Jonathan entered the woods, he spotted bees swarming over a hole in the ground. "Honey!" He reached out the end of his staff, dipped it into the hole, and brought up a portion of honeycomb. "God provides!" He ate and felt his strength increasing.

Men stopped and watched him, but made no move to take any of the honey.

"Eat!" Jonathan looked around at them, perplexed. "What's the matter with you?" He dipped his staff again and held it out to them. "The honey will strengthen you!"

"We can't!"

"Your father made the army take a strict oath that anyone who eats food today will be cursed. That is why everyone is weary and faint."

Jonathan went cold, and then hot. "My father has made trouble for us all!" Would he have to die for eating the honey? "A command like that only hurts us. See how refreshed I am now that I have eaten this little bit of honey. It is a gift from the Lord!"

"If we eat it, the king will have us killed."

He pressed them no further. His father would excuse him, but would not excuse others. "If the men had been allowed to eat freely from the food they found among our enemies, think how many more Philistines we could have killed!" All the Philistines would have been dead before the day was over.

Jonathan turned away and continued the chase. Those who could, followed.

✦ ✦ ✦

From Micmash to Aijalon, the Philistines fell. Many escaped because Saul's men were too exhausted from lack of food to follow after them. When the Hebrews came upon sheep, cattle, and calves, they fell upon them, slaughtering the animals in the field and cutting away chunks of flesh, their mouths dripping blood as they ate to satisfy their ravenous hunger.

The priest cried out, "Stop what you're doing! You're breaking the Law."

The men did not listen.

Saul built an altar and ordered the men to bring the animals there. "Kill them here, and drain the blood before you eat them. Do not sin against the Lord by eating meat with the blood still in it."

"Do not sin against the Lord." The priest ran, echoing the king's command. "You must not eat meat with blood still in it!"

Sickened, Jonathan turned away. It was too late to undo what the men had done.

Anxiety spread through the camp. The men who had followed Jonathan came to him. "We will say nothing of what you did in the forest."

Jonathan was troubled by their fear. Did they really think the king would kill his own son? Would he? Could he?

Saul summoned him. "So you disobey me again?"

Jonathan's stomach was a cold knot of fear. He felt sweat break out on the back of his neck. Had someone told the king about the honey? The king's advisors looked at Jonathan, their expressions closed, watchful. "You go out to war without my leave!"

Jonathan lifted his head. "God gave us victory."

"You might have been killed! What did you think you were doing, going out against the Philistines with only your armor bearer? Where is he?" Saul looked around. "Why isn't he at your side?"

"He's asleep." Jonathan bared his teeth in a forced grin. "It has been a long day, Father."

Saul laughed and pounded Jonathan's back. "My son! The warrior!" He looked at the men. "He climbs a cliff, kills more than a score of Philistines, all better equipped and more skilled than he, and then he sets the entire Philistine army on the run!" His eyes glowed as he looked at Jonathan. "You bring honor upon your father, the king."

Jonathan saw something dark in his father's praise. "The panic that came upon the Philistines was from the Lord, my king. It is the Lord who rescued Israel this day."

"Yes!" Saul pounded him again. "The Lord." He smiled at the others. "But we've kept them running, haven't we?" He went to a table and unrolled a map. "Let's chase the Philistines all night and plunder them until sunrise. Let's destroy every last one of them. Think of the wealth it will bring me!"

Jonathan thought that unwise. "The men are exhausted. And now that they have eaten, they will sleep as though drugged."

Saul glared at him. "The men will do what *I* say."

And perish for it! Jonathan held his tongue, hoping the advisors would speak sense.

Instead, they all agreed with the king. They said exactly what Saul wanted to hear. "We'll do whatever you think is best. We will go after them and be the richer for it."

Jonathan looked at Ahijah. "Shouldn't we inquire of the Lord?"

The priest took a nervous step forward. "Your son shows your great wisdom, my lord. Let's ask God first."

When the others agreed, Saul shrugged. "Should we go after the Philistines? Will You help us defeat them?"

Ahijah placed his hands over the Urim and Thummin and waited for God's answer.

Saul stood silent.

The men waited.

The Lord did not answer.

✦   ✦   ✦

The night seemed darker to Jonathan. Even as dawn came, he felt no lifting in his spirit. The sun rose and moved slowly across the sky, and with it the echoing words of the soldiers in the woods: *"Your father made the army take a strict oath . . . anyone who eats food today will be cursed."*

Jonathan bowed his face to the ground. *Lord, I took no such oath. I knew nothing about it! Am I still bound by it? Do You refuse to speak to the king because I sinned? Let it not be so. Don't let me again be the one to bring disaster upon the people!*

When he rose, he sat back on his heels. He knew what he must do.

Abner intercepted him. "What do you think you're doing?"

"I must speak with my father, the king."

"And confess about the honey?"

"You know—"

"Yes! I know. I know everything that happens among my men. I have to know!" He pulled Jonathan aside. "No one has said anything to the king. Nor will they."

"I've brought trouble upon him again."

"He made a hasty vow, Jonathan. Should that vow cost the people their prince?"

Jonathan tried to step around him.

Abner blocked his way, eyes flashing. "Do you think the Lord would want the death of His champion?"

Jonathan went hot. "The Lord needs no champion!"

Abner caught hold of Jonathan's arm, holding him back. "What glory would the Lord receive from your death?"

When Jonathan turned away, he saw his father watching from the entrance of his tent.

Eyes dark, Saul came outside and shouted orders. "Something's wrong!" He looked at Abner. "I want all my army commanders to come here."

The men gathered quickly and stood before him.

Saul looked at each of them. "We must find out what sin was committed today."

Jonathan was afraid. Never had he seen such a look on

his father's face. The king's eyes burned with suspicion. *Does my father now see me as his enemy?* He felt sick.

"Jonathan and I will stand over here, and all of you stand over there."

Jonathan took his place at the king's side. Would his father kill him?

"We want a king like the nations around us!"

Jonathan's heart began to pound heavily. He had heard stories about the surrounding nations, how they executed their own sons to maintain their power. Some even sacrificed them on the city walls to please their gods. Sweat broke out on his face. *Will my father kill me, Lord? Not my father.*

"I vow by the name of the Lord who rescued Israel that the sinner will surely die, even if it is my own son Jonathan!"

Jonathan received his answer, but he could not believe it. *No. He cannot have changed so much.* He looked at Abner, then at the others. The men all stared straight ahead, not meeting his eyes. Not a man spoke a word.

Frustrated, Saul summoned the entire army. "Someone will tell me!" When the men were gathered, the king prayed loudly. "O Lord, God of Israel, please show us who is guilty and who is innocent."

Jonathan looked at his father. He didn't know what to do. If he confessed now, would his father break his vow or keep it? Either way, Jonathan had put his father in an untenable position yet again. Fear shook him, for no good could come from this day!

The priest cast lots. Men and their units were found innocent.

Jonathan felt his father's tension grow with each pass-

ing moment. Moisture beaded the king's forehead. Jonathan could smell the rank sweat of fear. *He knows! He's
afraid it's me! He doesn't know what to do! He won't kill
me. He loves me. He can't kill his own son.*

Saul held out a trembling hand. "Now cast lots again
and choose between me and Jonathan."

Ahijah did so. He looked up, relieved. "It's Jonathan,
my lord."

When his father turned, eyes blazing, Jonathan was
shocked to see relief in his eyes, even as they welled with
tears of fury. "Tell me what you have done!"

"I tasted a little honey," Jonathan admitted. "It was
only a little bit on the end of my stick. Does that deserve
death?"

"Yes, Jonathan," Saul said, "you must die! May God
strike me and even kill me if you do not die for this." Saul
drew his sword.

Jonathan gaped, too shocked to move.

"No!" Officers moved quickly between king and prince.
"Jonathan has won this great victory for Israel. Should he
die? *Far from it!*"

Men shouted from every side.

Abner spoke louder than the rest. "As surely as the
Lord lives, not one hair on his head will be touched, for
God helped him do a great deed today. You cannot do this,
Saul!"

Jonathan cringed. He saw his father's wrath evaporate.
He looked this way and that. Finally, Saul slid his sword
back into its scabbard. "My hand will not be raised
against my own son." He put his hand on Jonathan's
shoulder and dismissed the army.

As they walked away, Saul took his hand away and

went inside the tent. Jonathan followed. He wanted to beg forgiveness. Abner and the advisors stood around him.

Saul faced them. "God has destroyed the wheat harvest, but other crops will soon be ready for harvest, and an army needs provisions." He did not look at Jonathan. "We will not pursue the Philistines. We will withdraw to our own land. Tell your units to break camp. We leave within the hour."

"Father—"

"Not now. We will talk later, on the way home."

When the army was on the move, Jonathan walked beside his father. "I'm sorry."

"Sorry." Saul's tone was flat. He stared straight ahead. "Samuel is against me. Is my own son to be my enemy as well?"

Jonathan's heart sank and tears welled. "Had I known of your vow, I never would have eaten the honey."

Saul glanced at him and then looked ahead again. "Jonathan, you are either with me or you are against me. Which is it?"

Never had words hurt so much. "No one is more loyal to you than I."

"It may seem so to you, but if you continue to act on your own as you did at Geba and now Micmash, you will split the nation. Is that what you want? To remove the crown from my head and have Samuel place it on your own?"

"No!" Jonathan stopped and turned to him. *"No!"*

"Keep walking!"

Jonathan fell into step beside him. His father spoke again, without looking at him. "They all stood against me in order to protect you."

Jonathan could not deny it. Men were easily swayed by an act of courage, but it was God—not he—who had brought the victory. "I only meant to rally the men."

"And me?"

Had his actions brought shame upon his father? What could he say to make amends if that were so?

"Samuel said God has already chosen another to be king." Saul looked at Jonathan, frowning. "Is it you?"

Crushed, Jonathan spoke, his voice choked with emotion. "Father, no! You are king of Israel. My hand will never be raised against you!"

Saul's eyes cleared of suspicion. He put his hand on Jonathan's shoulder and squeezed. "We must protect one another, my son. Like it or not, our lives are in peril. Not just our lives, but those of your brothers as well. If anyone takes the crown from us, Malkishua, Abinadab, Ishbosheth, and your sisters will be killed so that my line will be ended. Do you understand? It is the way of kings to destroy all their enemies, even the children that might grow up to come against them."

He squeezed Jonathan's shoulder again and released him. "Don't trust anyone, Jonathan. We have enemies all around us. Enemies everywhere."

It was true Israel was threatened from all sides. The Philistines were along the coast, Moab to the east, Ammon to the north, and the kings of Zobah to the south. It seemed the entire world wanted to destroy God's people! And the fastest way to scatter an army was to kill the king.

But his father seemed to think there were enemies among their own people as well.

"We will unite the tribes, Father. We will teach them to trust in the Lord our God."

Saul was looking ahead. "You will be at my right hand." He kept walking. "We will build a dynasty."

Jonathan glanced at him. Samuel had said—

Saul made a fist. "I will hold on to my power." His arm jerked as he spoke to himself in a low, hard voice. "I will hold on to my power. I will." He let his hand drop to his side and his chin went up. "I will!"

THREE

SAMUEL came to the king with a commandment from the Lord: Go out and destroy the Amalekites who had waylaid and murdered the defenseless Israelite stragglers who had come out of Egypt.

"Here is a chance for glory!" Saul slapped Jonathan on the back. "God will surely bless us!"

And they did have victory. But Jonathan worried, warning his father not to delay in obeying every instruction Samuel had given. "He said to destroy everything!"

"King Agag is your father's trophy." Abner raised his goblet to King Saul. "He is more use to us alive than dead. When all Israel sees him humbled, they will know the only man they need fear is King Saul!"

Jonathan looked between them. "Kill *every* Amalekite, Samuel said, and the animals as well."

His father clapped him on the shoulder. "Celebrate, Jonathan. Stop worrying so much."

"The Law says to love the Lord your God with all your heart—"

"—mind, soul, and strength." Saul waved his hand. "Yes, I know the Law, too."

Did he? He had never written the Law in his own hand, nor listened for long when Jonathan read it to him. "You have not completed—"

"Enough!" Saul slammed his goblet down. Men looked their way. Saul waved magnanimously. "Eat! Drink! Be merry!" He leaned toward Jonathan and spoke in a hoarse whisper. "Take your gloom elsewhere." When Jonathan started to rise, Saul grabbed his arm. "Look around you,

Jonathan." Wine splashed from his goblet as he swept his arm wide. "See how happy the men are. We must keep them happy!"

Jonathan saw the fear in his father's eyes, but knew it was misplaced. "It is the Lord we must please, Father. *The Lord*."

Saul released him and waved him away.

Jonathan went outside and sat staring out over the hills.

What would Samuel say when he came?

He covered his head, ashamed.

✦   ✦   ✦

King Saul led the army to Carmel, taking with him the best of the Amalekites' sheep and goats, cattle, fat calves and lambs. He ordered a monument erected in his own honor. Continuing the celebrations, he displayed the captive King Agag for all to see as he led the army back to Gilgal.

Samuel came to meet him there.

"May the Lord bless you!" Saul opened his arms wide. "I have carried out the Lord's command."

"Then what is all the bleating of sheep and goats and the lowing of cattle I hear?"

Jonathan cringed at the fierce anger in Samuel's voice.

His father glanced at the officers and leaders. "Come! You need refreshment." Saul led the way to his tent, leaving the others behind.

Samuel entered the king's tent. Saul poured wine, but Samuel would not take it.

Flustered, Saul explained. "It's true that the army spared the best of the sheep, goats, and cattle." He looked at Jonathan. Eyes flickering, he turned back to Samuel and added quickly, "But they are going to sacrifice them to the Lord your God. We have destroyed everything else."

"Stop!" Samuel cried out. He bowed his head and raised his hands to cover his ears.

King Saul took a step back, his face ashen. "Leave us."

Jonathan went willingly, fear knotting his stomach. He kept watch at the entrance of the king's quarters. He could hear every word.

Samuel spoke. "Listen to what the Lord told me last night!"

"What did He tell you?"

"Although you may think little of yourself, are you not the leader of the tribes of Israel? The Lord has anointed you king of Israel. And the Lord sent you on a mission and told you, 'Go and completely destroy the sinners, the Amalekites, until they are all dead.' Why haven't you obeyed the Lord? Why did you rush for the plunder and do what was evil in the Lord's sight?"

Jonathan's heart pounded faster with each word the prophet spoke.

"But I did obey the Lord!"

Don't argue, Father. Confess!

"I carried out the mission He gave me."

Father, don't lie!

"I brought back King Agag, but I destroyed everyone else. Then my troops brought in the best of the sheep, goats, cattle, and plunder to sacrifice to the Lord your God in Gilgal."

The heat of shame filled Jonathan's face as he listened to his father's lies and excuses.

Samuel raised his voice. "What is more pleasing to the Lord: your burnt offerings and sacrifices or your obedi-

ence to His voice? Listen! Obedience is better than sacrifice, and submission is better than offering the fat of rams.
Rebellion is as sinful as witchcraft, and stubbornness as
bad as worshiping idols. So because you have rejected the
command of the Lord, He has rejected you as king."

Saul cried out in fear, "All right! I admit it. Yes, I have
sinned. I have disobeyed your instructions and the Lord's
command, for I was afraid of the people and did what they
demanded. But now, please forgive my sin and come back
with me so that I may worship the Lord."

Jonathan held his head and paced, cold sweat beading.
It wasn't God his father feared, but men. *Lord, have mercy.*
Lord, have mercy.

"I will not go back with you!" Samuel's voice came
closer to the opening of the tent. He was leaving. "Since
you have rejected the Lord's command, He has rejected
you as king of Israel."

Jonathan heard a struggle and the sound of tearing
cloth, and his heart stopped. He opened the curtain and
saw his father on his knees, clutching at the prophet's torn
robe, his face ashen, his eyes wild with fear.

Samuel stared down at him in anguish. "The Lord
has torn the kingdom of Israel from you today and has
given it to someone else—one who is better than you."
Samuel raised his head and closed his eyes. "And He
who is the Glory of Israel will not lie, nor will He
change His mind, for He is not human that He should
change His mind!"

"I know I have sinned," Saul moaned. "But please, at
least honor me before the elders of my people and before
Israel by coming back with me so that I may worship the
Lord your God."

Heart sinking, Jonathan took his hand from the curtain. His father was more afraid of the men who waited outside than he was of the Lord God who held a man's life in the palm of His mighty hand.

Samuel came outside with Saul. If anyone noticed his torn robe, no one spoke of it. Saul pretended everything was all right. He talked, smiled, his gaze moving from one leader to another.

Jonathan's body was taut. He waited. *God does not change His mind.*

"Bring King Agag to me," Samuel said.

Everyone looked at Saul. "Go!" the king said. "Do as he says."

A few moments later, Jonathan saw the Amalekite king walking in front of the guards, head high. Clearly, he thought all the bitterness of death was behind him and he was safe in Saul's care. He gave a nod to Saul and then lifted his head as he looked at Samuel. Was he waiting for an introduction?

Samuel drew the sword from King Saul's scabbard. "As your sword has killed the sons of many mothers, now your mother will be childless." He raised the sword high and brought it down before the Amalekite could move.

Agag's lifeless body crumpled to the ground, his skull cleaved open.

Everyone talked at once. Saul grabbed his sword and jerked it free. He shouted for his officers to dismiss their divisions. They could go home. The Amalekites were no longer a threat. He called to Abner. "We are going home to Gibeah."

Jonathan followed after Samuel. They walked together in silence for a long while, and then Samuel stopped and looked at him. "The Lord is grieved that He made Saul king over Israel." He stood silent and erect.

Jonathan felt the rejection as acutely as though he were responsible for all of his father's sins. His shoulders heaved. Tears streamed down his cheeks.

Samuel stepped forward and grasped Jonathan's arm. "The Lord is your salvation. Blessed be the name of the Lord."

"So be it." Jonathan choked out the words.

Samuel's hold loosened. "I'm going home to Ramah." He walked away, bent in sorrow.

Though he didn't know it then, it was the last time Jonathan would ever see his beloved mentor.

+   +   +

Jonathan saw his father change after that day. In the first of his strange bouts of rage, Saul held his head and ranted. "I will not listen! I will not!" Grabbing a goblet, he threw it against a wall. "Why should I listen to you?" He overturned a table.

Men watched from doorways, ducking back when the king turned in their direction. Jonathan, keeping watch outside his father's chamber, sent them away. He didn't want anyone to see the king like this. The whole of Israel would be in confusion—and easy prey to enemies—if word spread that Saul was mad.

"He says he'll end my dynasty!" Saul's eyes blazed wildly. He ripped his tunic, mumbling. Sweat dripped. Saliva bubbled. "Why should I listen to you when you hate me?" He tore the turban from his head. "Get away from me! Leave me alone!" He swung around. "Abner!"

Abner grabbed Jonathan's arm, his eyes wide with

fear. "We must do something for your father or all will be lost."

"I don't know what to do. Talking to him does no good."

"Abner!"

"Speak with your mother," Abner whispered, his voice urgent. "Sometimes a woman knows ways to soothe a man's temper." He turned and entered the king's chamber. "Yes, my lord?"

"Have you sent someone to watch Samuel?"

"Yes, my lord."

"I want someone keeping an eye on him at all times. I want to know every move he makes . . ."

Jonathan went to his mother. She was in new quarters, away from the king, who had taken a concubine. A servant led him into the room and he saw his mother working at her loom. She glanced up with a smile that quickly turned to a frown. "Sit. Tell me what troubles you."

He tried to find words. Looking at the multicolored sash she was making, he forced a smile.

She followed his gaze and ran her hand over her work. "A gift for your father."

"He will wear it proudly."

"Did he send you?"

"No."

She folded her hands. "I've heard about his spells, though you and Abner and the rest try to keep it secret."

Jonathan stood and went to the grated window. He didn't want to imagine what could happen if word spread. His father was at his most vulnerable.

"Tell me what's happening, Jonathan. I have been shut away here with my servants."

"Some men say Father is possessed of an evil spirit." He thought it more likely Saul's guilt racked his mind. "But I think it's something else."

"What?"

"Sometimes, when I hear what he's mumbling, I wonder if God isn't trying to speak to him, and he's hardening his heart and mind against Him." He turned. "I don't know what to do, Mother."

His mother sat with her head down. Then she rose and came to stand beside him at the window. She looked out for a moment and then faced him. "Your father has always loved the sound of a harp. Perhaps if you found someone to play for him when he suffers these spells—" she put her hand gently on his arm—"he might be soothed."

+   +   +

Jonathan mentioned his mother's suggestion to his father's servants, who in turn presented the idea to the king. "All right," Saul said. "Find me someone who plays well, and bring him here."

One of the king's servants sent by the tribe of Judah spoke up. "One of Jesse's sons from Bethlehem is a talented harp player. Not only that—he is a brave warrior, a man of war, and has good judgment. He is also a fine-looking young man, and the Lord is with him."

Saul ordered he be sent for.

The boy arrived a few days later with a donkey loaded with bread, a skin of wine, and a goat—all gifts so that the boy's provisions would cost the king nothing. That night, when an evil spirit came upon the king, the musician was summoned from his bed.

At the first sounds of the harp, the king calmed.

"The Lord is my shepherd," the boy sang softly,
slowly.

> *"I have all that I need.*
> *He lets me rest in green meadows;*
> *He leads me beside peaceful streams."*

The king sat, pressing his fingers against his forehead.

> *"He renews my strength.*
> *He guides me along right paths,*
> *bringing honor to His name.*
> *Even when I walk*
> *through the darkest valley,*
> *I will not be afraid,*
> *for You are close beside me."*

Saul leaned back against the cushions as the boy sang.
Jonathan watched his father relax and close his eyes. The
boy had a clear, pleasing voice, but it was the words of his
song that brought peace into the king's chamber.

A man close by whispered, "The boy sings praises to
the king."

"No." Jonathan looked at the boy. "He sings praises to
God."

The song continued, filling the chamber with words
and sound so free and sweet, violent men were calmed.

> *"Your rod and your staff*
> *protect and comfort me.*
> *You prepare a feast for me*
> *in the presence of my enemies.*

You honor me by anointing my head with oil.
  My cup overflows with blessings.
Surely Your goodness and unfailing love will pursue me
  all the days of my life,
and I will live in the house of the Lord forever."

As the last words and chords of the harp quivered to silence, Jonathan sighed. Oh, to have such confidence in God! He longed to feel at peace with the Lord. His soul yearned for such a relationship.

"Sing another." King Saul waved his hand.

The boy plucked at his harp. "The heavens proclaim the glory of God," he sang.

> *"The skies display His craftsmanship.*
> *Day after day they continue to speak;*
>   *night after night they make Him known. . . ."*

"Look," someone whispered. "The king sleeps."

Jonathan had not seen his father this relaxed in weeks. His own muscles loosened. Everyone in the chamber seemed soothed. When the boy finished his song, the king roused slightly.

"Sing another," Abner told the boy.

The boy sang of the Law this time. The Law is perfect! The Lord is trustworthy. The Law is right and true! The Law carries fearful warning and great reward! Follow it and live!

Listen, Father! Drink it in as you sleep.

> *"May the words of my mouth*
>   *and the mediation of my heart*

be pleasing to You,
   O Lord, my rock and my redeemer."

The boy bowed his head, plucked the last few chords,
and then sat in silence.

Lord, here is one who shares my thoughts.

Saul awakened slowly. "I am pleased with the boy.
Send word to his father that I want him to stay here in my
service. He can be one of my armor bearers."

"Yes, my lord. I will see to it immediately."

The king went to his bedchamber.

Jonathan called to the Judean servant who was leading
the boy outside. "Give the boy quarters inside the palace
so that he may be quickly summoned should the king
need him."

The servant bowed.

"And give him finer garments. He serves the king
now—not a flock of sheep."

✦   ✦   ✦

The Philistines gathered forces at Socoh in the territory of
Judah and made camp at Ephes-dammin. And once more
King Saul and Jonathan went to war. Battle lines were
drawn: the Philistines on one hill, and the Israelites on the
other, with the valley of Elah between them.

Where once Israel had fought boldly and routed the
Philistines, they now were rooted in fear. Twice a day,
once in the morning and later in the afternoon, the
Philistine king sent forth his champion, Goliath, a warrior who was over nine feet tall. The man was a giant
who wore a bronze helmet and coat of mail and bronze
leg armor. What sort of man could wear over one hun-

dred pounds of protective gear and still move so easily?
Goliath's shield bearer was not much smaller and led the
way as Goliath strode confidently into the center of the
valley.

Day after day, Saul and Jonathan and all the rest
quaked at the sight of him. They listened and trembled
at the sound of the giant's deep voice booming across
the valley in defiance. Israel's courage waned before the
Philistine's arrogance. The enemy lined up on the far
hill facing them and delighted in their humiliation.

"Why are you all coming out to fight?" Goliath
roared. "I am the Philistine champion, but you are only
the servants of Saul. Choose one man to come down here
and fight me! If he kills me, then we will be your slaves."

The Philistine troops hooted and laughed.

Goliath banged his shield with his sword. "But if I kill
him, you will be our slaves!"

The Philistines raised their swords and spears and
roared their approval. "Where is your champion?" they
chanted. "Send out your champion!"

Saul retreated to his tent. "How long must I bear this?"
he moaned, covering his ears. "Who will fight for *me*?"

"Jonathan is our champion." One of the advisors looked
at him.

Jonathan went cold at the thought of facing Goliath. He
couldn't go out against that giant. The man was half again
his size!

"No!" Saul turned. "I won't have my son slaughtered
before my eyes."

Abner stepped forward. "Offer a reward to any man
who will go forth as our champion."

Saul scowled. "What reward would entice a man to certain death?"

His officers all spoke at once:

"Great wealth."

"Give him one of your daughters in marriage."

"Exempt his family from taxes. All these would be his if he can silence that monster!"

"*If*—" Saul wiped the sweat from his face. "There is not a man in our kingdom who can stand against Goliath of Gath!"

"Not to mention the others."

"What others?" Saul's eyes darted from man to man.

"Saph, for one." Abner looked grim.

Another spoke. "And Goliath has a brother equally mighty."

"There are at least four warriors who are said to be descended from Gath."

"Even if we found a man who could kill the Philistine champion, my lord, can their king be trusted to submit? Never!"

"He will send another and another."

"Now you tell me." Saul sank into despair.

Weeks passed, and each morning, the armies again went out into battle position, facing one another across the valley. Each day, the Israelites shouted their war cry. And each day, Goliath came out mocking Israel and their God.

"I defy the armies of Israel today! Send me a man who will fight me!"

No one went out to answer his challenge.

Jonathan wondered how much more the men could bear before they began to desert, going back to hiding out in caves and cisterns. *Lord, help us! Send us a champion who can wipe the sweat of fear from our brows! God, do not desert us now!*

"What's going on down there?" Abner growled, as a disturbance broke out a short distance away.

"Just some men arguing."

Jonathan grew angry. "The Philistines will enjoy that! See to those men!" The last thing they needed was their own men fighting among themselves. Let them focus their anger upon the enemy and not their own brothers. A messenger ran to the ranking officer. A few minutes later, the officer came with his hand on a boy's shoulder.

"This boy is making trouble. He wants to speak with the king."

"You're the harpist." Jonathan frowned. What was he doing here?

"Yes, my lord."

"Come with me."

Saul turned, agitated, as they entered his tent.

Jonathan lifted his hand from the boy's shoulder. Released, the boy stepped forward boldly. "My father, Jesse, sent me with provisions for my older brothers. Eliab, Abinadab, and Shimea came to fight for the king."

"Leave the provisions and go home." Saul waved him away. "This is no place for you."

"Don't worry about this Philistine." The boy took another step forward. "I'll go fight him!"

The military advisors stared. "You?" One of them laughed. "The foolishness of youth. The Philistine is almost twice your size."

Jonathan saw something in the shepherd boy's eyes that gave him hope. "Let him speak!"

The men fell silent. Perhaps they remembered that

Jonathan had not been much older than this boy when he climbed the cliff to Micmash and God used him to rout the entire Philistine army! The boy looked at Jonathan, eyes glowing with recognition and respect.

Saul looked the boy over. "You think you can become Israel's champion?" He shook his head. "Don't be ridiculous! There's no way you can fight this Philistine and possibly win! You're only a boy, and he's been a man of war since his youth."

Flushed with anger, the boy would not be turned away. "I have been taking care of my father's sheep and goats. When a lion or a bear comes to steal a lamb from the flock, I go after it with a club and rescue the lamb from its mouth." He reached out as though demonstrating. "If the animal turns on me, I catch it by the jaw and club it to death." He hit his fist against the palm of his hand.

The advisors snickered. Jonathan silenced them with a look.

"I have done this to both lions and bears, and I'll do it to this pagan Philistine, too, for he has defied the armies of the living God!"

The boy understood what the king and advisors didn't. The monster not only mocked the king and his army, but insulted the Lord God of heaven and earth!

"The Lord who rescued me from the claws of the lion and the bear will rescue me from this Philistine!"

Saul looked at Jonathan. Jonathan nodded. Surely the Lord Himself was with the boy as the Lord had been with his father at Jabesh-gilead and with him when he climbed the cliffs at Micmash. How else could the boy be filled with such fire and confidence?

"All right, go ahead," Saul said. "And may the Lord be with you! Bring my armor!" Saul dressed the boy in his own tunic and coat of arms. He put the bronze helmet on his head. The boy sank lower with each piece added. Finally Saul handed over his sword. "Go. And the Lord be with you."

Jonathan frowned. The boy could hardly walk in the king's armor. The sword bumped clumsily against his thighs. When he tried to draw it from the scabbard, he almost dropped it.

Abner stared, appalled. "Will we send a child to do a man's work?"

Jonathan glared. "Would you have the king go? I'm too much of a coward! How about you, Abner? Are you willing to go?" He looked round at the others. "Is any one of us courageous enough to stand and fight Goliath?"

The boy handed the sword back to King Saul. "I can't go in these." He removed the helmet and armor and fine tunic. "I'm not used to them." He pulled a sling from his belt and went outside.

All the men talked at once.

Jonathan went out and saw the boy heading for a dry creek bed. He stooped and weighed stones in his hand. He decided on a round, smooth stone and placed it in the pouch of his shepherd's bag.

"What's your name?"

The boy straightened and bowed his head in respect to Jonathan. "David, my lord prince, son of Jesse of Bethlehem."

"You do know Goliath has a brother?"

"Does he?" David selected another stone.

"There are said to be three other giants of Gath among the Philistine ranks."

David picked up three more stones, added them to his shepherd's bag. "Is there anything else I need to know?"

Jonathan felt an assurance he hadn't felt since Micmash. "God is with you!"

David bowed low, and then walked toward the valley floor.

Jonathan ran back up the hill to stand with his father and watch.

Saul stood, shoulders slumped, dejected. "I have sent that boy out there to die."

"Let's watch and see what the Lord will do."

The Hebrew warriors moved to stand in battle array, murmuring as David walked down into the valley with nothing but his sling, a pouch of five smooth stones, and his shepherd's staff.

A commotion started in the line as David's relatives saw him striding down the hill. "What's he doing? Get out of there!" The officers ordered silence.

Jonathan looked down into the valley again. He prayed fervently. "God, be with him as You were with me at Micmash. Let all Israel see what the Lord can do!"

Goliath and his armor bearer advanced, shouting in disgust. "Am I a dog, that you come at me with a stick? May Dagon curse you!" The Philistine spat curses by all the gods of Philistia on the boy and all Israel while the Philistine warriors laughed and banged their shields.

Jonathan clenched his hand.

"Come over here, boy!" Goliath sneered. "I'll give your flesh to the birds and wild animals!"

"We come to this!" Abner groaned.

Jonathan waited and watched, praying as David stood straight and faced their enemy, his youthful voice carrying. "You come to me with sword, spear, and javelin, but I come to you in the name of the Lord of Heaven's Armies—the God of the armies of Israel, whom you have defied."

Goliath roared with laughter, the Philistine warriors joining him.

David walked forward. "Today the Lord will conquer you, and I will kill you and cut off your head. And then I will give the dead bodies of your men to the birds and wild animals, and the whole world will know that *there is a God in Israel!*"

David put a stone in his sling and ran toward Goliath.

Jonathan stepped forward. Could he hear the *whir* of the shepherd's sling? Or was it his own pulse that hummed in his ears, his heart pounding with every step David took? The boy's arm shot out and the sling dropped in his hand.

Goliath staggered back, a stone embedded in his forehead. Blood gushed down his face. He spread his feet, trying to keep his balance. Then he toppled like a tree.

Both armies stood in stunned silence. Goliath's armor bearer fled from David, who raised Goliath's sword and, with a shout, brought it down. Grabbing Goliath's severed head by the hair, the shepherd boy held it up for all to see. *"For the Lord!"*

Exultant, Jonathan drew his sword and held it high, answering. *"For the Lord and Israel!"*

Fear vanquished, King Saul and Jonathan led the charge, and once more the mighty Philistines fled in terror before the army of the Lord.

✦ ✦ ✦

When the battle was won, Jonathan searched for David. "Where is he?"

Saul shook his head. "I don't know. When Abner brought him to me, the boy was still holding Goliath's head! But he's gone."

"His name is David, Father. He is the youngest son of Jesse of Bethlehem."

"I know. The same boy who has been in my household for months strumming his harp and singing in my chambers." Saul laughed a bit uneasily. "Who knew he had such a fierce heart!"

"He fights for the Lord and his king." Jonathan laughed with excitement. "The whole world will hear of what he did today. I've got to find him." He wanted to know more about this boy God had used so mightily.

"Abner is finding quarters for him," Saul called after him. "We will want him close."

"He'll make a fine bodyguard!" Jonathan raised his sword in the air and went off to find him.

When Jonathan spotted David among the men of Judah and shouted, David turned. Jonathan spread his arms and gave an exuberant cry of victory.

David bowed low. "My lord prince."

Jonathan grabbed the boy's arm, shaking him slightly. "I knew the Lord was with you!"

"As He was with you at Micmash, my prince. My brothers talked of nothing else for months!"

"Come. Walk with me." David fell into step beside him. "You will be handsomely rewarded for what you did today."

"I ask for nothing."

"You will have a command of your own."

David stopped, his eyes going wide. "But I know nothing of leading men."

Jonathan laughed and ruffled David's curly hair. "I will teach you everything I know."

"But I'm only a shepherd."

"Not anymore." Jonathan grinned. "You will write songs that lead us into battle."

"But it was the Lord who won the victory. The Lord was my rock. The Lord delivered me from the hand of Goliath!"

Jonathan faced him. "Yes! And it is such words from your lips that will turn men's hearts to God." Jonathan would no longer be a lone voice in the king's court. "They saw." Here was a boy who believed as he did. "They will listen to you."

David shook his head. "May those who witnessed what happened today know they can trust in the Lord!"

"I know what you felt when you went out there. I felt it once when I climbed the cliffs at Micmash." Jonathan looked up. "I would give anything to feel the presence of the Lord again." Anything and everything!

"I dreamed of fighting for King Saul, but my brothers just laughed at me."

"They won't laugh anymore."

"No, but I'm not sure they would follow me either."

"Would they follow a king's son?"

"Of course."

"Then we will make you one."

"What do you mean?"

Jonathan stripped off his breastplate and tossed it.

David caught it against his chest and stumbled back. Jonathan yanked his fine tunic off and thrust it at David. "Put it on."

David stammered.

"Do as I say." Jonathan removed his sword and scabbard and fixed it around David's waist. Last, he gathered up his bow and quiver of arrows and gave them to him as well. "We are now brothers."

David blinked. "But what can I give you?"

"Your sling."

Fumbling, David finally managed to yank it from his belt. He held it out to Jonathan, flustered. "You do me too much honor, my prince."

"Do I?" Of all the people he had met since his father became king of Israel, he had never wanted one to be even his friend. He wanted David to be his brother.

"You are the crown prince, heir to King Saul's throne."

If only my father had a heart like this boy. What a king he would be!

Jonathan clasped David's hand. "From this day forth, you are my brother. My soul is knit to yours in love. I swear before the Lord our God, my hand will never be raised against you."

David's eyes shone with tears. "Nor mine against you!"

Jonathan turned David toward camp. He slapped his back and gave him a playful shove. "Come. We have plans to make! We must drive God's enemies from the land!"

✦   ✦   ✦

"Promote a boy above others twice his age and skill?" Saul stared at Jonathan, incredulous. "Are you mad?"

"Why not? Am I not a commander? I've already seen to it, Father."

"You are *my son*, the prince of Israel! He is nothing more than a shepherd boy who had a little good luck with sling and stone!"

Good luck? "God was with him yesterday, Father." When his father scowled, Jonathan looked at Abner and the officers and advisors. "Is there any man here who would argue that David is our champion? We can't leave him without distinction." They were silent. "Say something. Or are you afraid to give sound advice to the king?" Jonathan turned away in disgust. "Can we talk alone, Father? Let's walk through the camp."

The king went outside with him. Men bowed as they walked among the tents. "Every man here speaks about how David went into the valley of death and slew the giant! Honor him, Father. Let the nations hear how one Hebrew shepherd boy is better than an army of Philistines!"

Saul spoke without turning his head. "What do you think, Abner?"

Abner was always near the king, guarding him.

"The men will be pleased, my lord."

Saul looked at Jonathan. "You don't merely admire his courage, do you? You like him."

"As should you, Father. The Lord used David to give you the battle. Keep him at your side, and we will have victory after victory."

Saul lowered his eyes and stiffened. His head came up. "Where is your sword?"

"I gave it to David."

"You did *what*?"

"I gave him my tunic also, and my bow and belt as well."

"What else did you give this upstart? Your seal ring?"

Jonathan face went hot. "Of course not!" He held his hand out to prove it. "I adopted him as my brother. I made him your son."

"Without asking me? What did you think you were doing to show him such honor!"

"Who better to show honor to, Father?" Jonathan went cold at his father's look. "You are the Lord's anointed. David fought for the glory of the One you serve."

Saul's eyes flashed. He opened his mouth and clenched his teeth, deciding not to say whatever had come into his mind. Breathing hard, he looked away, staring out over the thousands of tents. "He didn't fight for me."

"David is your servant."

"And best to keep him as such." A muscle tightened in Saul's jaw. He released his breath slowly. "But perhaps you're right. He has proved himself useful. Let's see what else he can do." He grew annoyed. "Hear how they all celebrate the victory! Do you remember how they called out *my* name in Jabesh-gilead?"

"And at Gilgal," Abner reminded him.

"May they never forget." Saul turned and walked away.

✦   ✦   ✦

Jonathan looked over his shoulder as he ran. He laughed. "Come on, little brother! You're faster than that!"

Straining, David gained a little. Jonathan stretched out, his feet flying across the ground. He leapt over several bushes and reached their goal well before David.

Gasping for air, David went to his knees. "You fly like an eagle!"

Panting, Jonathan bent at the waist, dragging in air. He grinned. "You almost beat me."

David lay back on the ground, arms spread. "Your legs are longer than mine."

"A rabbit can outrun a fox."

"If it's cunning. I'm not."

Lungs burning, Jonathan leaned against a boulder. "Excuses. Your legs will grow. Your strength will increase."

David laughed. "I'd be faster if my life depended on it."

Jonathan walked around, hands on his hips, waiting for his heart to slow and his body to cool. "You were much faster this time. One day you will keep up and maybe pass me by."

Sitting up, David dangled his hands between his knees. "You outrun me. You're an expert with bow and arrow. You can throw a spear twice as far as I can."

Someone shouted from a distance. Abner.

Jonathan gave David a hand up. He looped his hand around David's neck and rubbed his curly hair with his knuckles. "All in good time, my brother. All in good time."

✦   ✦   ✦

Women ran out to meet the returning warriors. They sang and danced around them, beating on tambourines and strumming lutes. They filled the air with songs of praise.

"See how they love you!" Jonathan laughed at the look on David's face as a girl danced by, flashing him a smile. "You're blushing!"

"I've never seen girls like these!" David watched them whirl around him. "They're beautiful!"

"Yes. They are." Jonathan admired several as he headed for the city gates.

Men, women, and children cheered as Saul led them into Gibeah. The king's household swarmed around Saul. Jonathan spotted his mother and grabbed David by the arm. "My father promised one of his daughters to the man who killed Goliath. You must meet my sisters. I recommend Merab. She's older than you, but much wiser than Michal."

David dug in his heels. "Jonathan, no! I am unworthy!"

"Better you than some old warrior with other wives and a harem of concubines!" He called out to his mother. She turned, smiling, stretching up to look for him. Jonathan pressed his way through the crowd, receiving congratulations and pats of welcome. When he finally reached her, he introduced David, "the giant killer."

"You are to be praised," she said.

Michal stared at David, moon-eyed and blushing.

David fidgeted. "What I did against Goliath is nothing compared to what the prince did at Micmash."

"My son is a very brave man." Jonathan's mother smiled.

"The bravest! It is an honor to serve King Saul and our prince."

"You are from Judah, are you not?"

"It was your recommendation that brought David to us, Mother."

"The boy who sings and plays the harp." She blinked, her face going pale.

David bowed in respect. "It will be my pleasure to sing for the king whenever he wishes. I am his servant."

"Father made David a ranking officer. He's earned other rewards as well." He looked at Merab. "He should be introduced to his future wife."

David cringed with embarrassment.

Jonathan's mother refused to meet his eyes. "Doesn't the Law state that men must take wives from their own tribes?"

Mortified, Jonathan stared. Had his mother meant to reprimand him and the king as well as insult David?

David stammered. "I-I would never count myself worthy to marry one of the king's daughters." Some of David's relatives called out to him, trying to reach him. "May I go, my lord?"

"Yes."

David ran.

Jonathan glared at his mother. "Did you mean to insult him?"

"I merely spoke the truth, Jonathan."

"The truth is that Father gave his oath. And who better for Merab than the champion of Israel, Mother?"

"Where are you going?"

"To find David and bring him back. He will be at the king's table tonight, along with all the high-ranking officers."

✦   ✦   ✦

The warriors dispersed. As they rejoined their families, Saul welcomed his relatives, officers, and advisors to a feast of celebration. Everyone ate his fill and talked of the battle. David sat across from Jonathan, facing the king. As the evening wore on, Saul leaned back against the wall and took a spear in his hand. His thumb rubbed against the shaft.

"David, will you sing for us? A song of deliverance."

A harp was handed from man to man until it reached David. He leaned over it and strummed softly. Men stopped talking to listen. The king closed his eyes and leaned back.

A servant picked his way across the room as David sang and leaned down to whisper to Jonathan. "Your mother, the queen, requests the pleasure of your company."

Surprised, Jonathan rose. His mother never interrupted him. "Father, may I be excused?"

"Go." Saul didn't open his eyes.

David continued to play.

The servant led him through the palace and into a large room where his mother sat weaving

Smiling, she rose and came to him. "About your friend, the shepherd boy."

Jonathan bristled. "*David*, Mother. His name is David. It's a name you should remember. I made a vow of friendship with him. He is my brother and due the same respect given me." When she said nothing, he felt impelled to go on. "Our friendship will solidify the ties between Judah and Benjamin."

"The tribes have been linked in friendship since the time of Joseph, my son. Judah, fourth son of Jacob, offered to take Benjamin's place as a slave in Egypt. I know our history, too, Jonathan. A rivalry grew between the tribes. When the people demanded a king, the Judeans were quick to remind us all that Jacob prophesied the scepter would never depart from their hands."

"Saul is king of Israel."

"And Judah bows down grudgingly."

"They stood with Saul at Jabesh-gilead. They celebrated his coronation at Gilgal. They were with us at Micmash and—" When she held up her hands, he stopped. Honor your father *and* mother, the Law said.

"You are too trusting, Jonathan."

He would never be able to explain to her how his soul was knit to David's. How could he when he didn't fully understand himself? And so, he used reason to try to convince her. "What better way to end rivalry than by the king's giving one of his daughters in marriage to his opponent's son?"

"The Law says—"

Jonathan sighed heavily. "I know, Mother. No one reminds my father of the Law more often than I. But even more important here is the fact that he made a public vow and must make good on it. A king is only as good as his promises."

Shaking her head, she walked to the window and looked up into the night sky. "Your father was not pleased by the songs the people sang as he entered the gates today."

"The people sang praises to their king."

She looked back at him. "And praised your friend more. 'Saul has killed his thousands, and David his ten thousands!' You should have seen your father's face."

"I didn't notice."

"No, you didn't. You need to notice, Jonathan. You need to keep close watch." She looked out the window again and spoke softly. "I fear a storm is brewing."

✦ ✦ ✦

Jonathan knew the truth of his mother's words when he
returned to the gathering and found everything in disar-
ray.

"Where's David?"

"Gone." Abner looked shaken.

Counselors clustered near Saul, talking in low voices.
"He oppresses me!" Saul shouted. "A boy, that's all he is!
Why do the people make so much of him?"

"What happened?"

"Your father lost his temper and threw a spear. That's
all. If he'd meant to kill David, he would have."

"He threw a spear at David? *Why*?"

"You know how things are."

Jonathan found David sitting at a fire among his relatives. When Jonathan entered the circle of light, cold eyes
fixed on him, but David rose quickly. "My prince!"

"I heard what happened."

David drew him away from the others. "Your father
tried to kill me. Twice he hurled a spear at me." David
gave a nervous laugh. "I thought it wise to leave before
the king pinned me to the wall."

"You've seen him when the evil spirit comes upon him.
It's why you were summoned to the palace."

"My songs did not soothe him tonight."

"Sometimes my father says and does things he would
never do if . . ." If what? If he was in his right mind? If he
was not tormented by guilt and fear? Jonathan could not
say these things to David. "He drank a lot of wine
tonight." He smiled wryly. "Maybe he thought you were
a Philistine." It was a bad joke.

They went up the ladder to the top of the wall and leaned against the railing, looking out over the land. Jonathan shook his head. "My father is a great man, David." He felt the leather case containing the Law thump against his chest. "But I wish he would listen to me."

"My father doesn't listen to me either. Nor do my uncles and brothers." David rested his chin on folded arms. "Even though I now outrank them."

"Every man in Israel should learn the Law. If they knew the Lord they served, they wouldn't be so afraid of the nations around us. They'd stop trying to live by the customs of our enemies." Did any of them realize that the Scriptures said God would detest them if they did that? Did they remember that God had warned them that the land itself would vomit them out?

"Maybe someday." David sighed. "My father said the Law is too much to learn and takes too much time away from the sheep."

Jonathan remembered how his own father had preferred plowing fields rather than digging into the Scriptures.

"I have often dreamed of going to Naioth." David smiled as he gazed at the night sky. "Those who attend the school of prophets are the most fortunate of men. What could be more exciting and wonderful than to spend your life reading and studying the Law?"

Jonathan looked at him. He had felt the bond between them at the valley of Elah. And it had grown stronger every day since. It was as though the Lord Himself had knit their hearts together. "I copied the Law at the school in Naioth."

David straightened, eyes wide. "You have a copy of the Law?"

Jonathan smiled and nodded slowly. He could see the sheen of excitement in David's eyes. Hadn't he felt the same thing: a hunger to know the Lord, an insatiable appetite to eat and drink the Word of God as his life's sustenence?

"All of it?" David stared in wonder.

"Every word of it." Jonathan took hold of the woven leather strap and drew the leather casing out from beneath his tunic. "I have part of it right here. Samuel oversaw my work to make certain every jot and tittle was exact."

David's eyes glowed. "Oh, what treasure you hold in your hand."

Jonathan pushed away from the wall. Smiling, he rested his hand on David's shoulder. He jerked his head. "What do you say we find ourselves a lamp and get my scrolls?"

They read the Law until they were too tired to see the words. Exhausted, David went out to his relatives and Jonathan returned to the palace. When he stretched out on his bed, he closed his eyes.

Finally, he had found someone who loved the Lord like Samuel did, a friend who was closer than a brother.

Jonathan smiled. He fell asleep exhausted. Content.

✦   ✦   ✦

The Philistines raided once again, and Saul sent David out to fight. Jonathan heard reports of David's success, and was pleased. Jonathan fought well also and drove the Philistines off tribal lands. Returning to Gibeah, he dined with his father.

"I heard David had another victory."

Saul's mouth was flat and hard. "Yes."

"Have the wedding arrangements been made?"

Saul was eating grapes, the muscles in his jaw bunching hard as he ground his teeth. "I'm still thinking about it."

Jonathan lost his appetite. "You gave your oath. The man who killed Goliath was to have wealth—"

"He is growing wealthy on plunder."

"Tax exemptions for his family—"

"So Jesse sends me a few sheep; why should I decline?"

"And your daughter in marriage."

"I offered him Merab, and he declined."

"He felt unworthy."

Saul gave a harsh laugh. "Or that impudent Judean thinks my daughter's not good enough for him."

Jonathan stared. "You know that's not true."

"David!" Saul spat the word as though it were a foul taste in his mouth. "So much humility!" He sneered and ripped a hunk of meat from the roasted lamb. "I have given Merab to Adriel of Meholah. She leaves day after tomorrow."

Jonathan felt the words like a punch in his stomach. "When was this decision made?"

"What does it matter to you when the decision was made? I am the king!" He threw the meat back onto the platter. "Judah is already an ally." He wiped his greasy hands on a cloth. "Meholah's clan was in question. They are now allies. It was a good decision."

Jonathan was too angry to speak.

His father looked at him. "Do not try me, Jonathan. I know David is your friend, but I understand our people better than you do! I must make alliances."

"You would have made an alliance with Judah by giv-

ing Merab to David. Do you think they will be pleased
that you've forgotten the promises you made at the valley
of Elah?"

Saul's face reddened. "They know I offered Merab to
him. I kept my promise."

Jonathan knew he could not let the subject go. Bridges
had to be built, not torn down, between the tribes. He
waited for his father to finish his meal and drink some
wine before he broached it again. "Michal is in love with
David."

His younger sister would not make as good a wife as
Merab, but what she lacked in sense she made up for in
beauty. The marriage would bring Benjamin and David
together, and if his sister bore David's sons, they would be
added to Saul's household. But most important, the marriage would confirm the king's honor.

"She is?"

"She told me today that he is the most handsome man in
all Israel."

Saul chewed, eyes gleaming. He made a gruff sound and
drank more wine. "What's to keep him from declining
Michal as he declined Merab?"

"He won't if you make it clear you think him worthy to
be your son. He paid the bride price when he killed Goliath."

"The bride price." Saul raised his head. "I had not
thought about that."

"So you will offer Michal."

"Of course." Saul plucked some grapes and tossed one
into his mouth. He leaned back, a smug smile curving his
lips.

✦   ✦   ✦

David returned to Gibeah. Jonathan was kept so busy with matters of state that he had no time to see him. And when he did, David was preparing to leave again. "Pray for me, my friend!" David clasped Jonathan's arms in greeting. He was trembling with excitement. "I have just spoken to several of the king's attendants and I may become your brother yet!"

"You are already my brother." Jonathan was delighted his father had followed through with his decision to give Michal to David.

David released him and they walked together. "I'm leaving in an hour."

"Leaving? For where?"

"The king announced the bride price for your sister Michal. And I have until the new moon festival."

"David!" Jonathan called before he went far. "What price did the king set?"

"One hundred foreskins!"

One hundred kills—and proof they were uncircumcised Philistines. Jonathan was dismayed, for it was another indication that his father was adopting the customs of surrounding nations. The Egyptians lopped off hands and collected them as trophies to prove how many they killed. The Philistines took heads. Jonathan wondered if his father understood that he might be sending David to his death. And if Israel lost their champion, what then? Would they lose their faith as well? By all that was right, Michal already belonged to David because of the king's promise.

But maybe his father was right. David was eager to prove himself worthy.

Lord, protect him. Go before him and be his rear guard. And may Michal prove herself a worthy bride when David returns!

✦   ✦   ✦

Jonathan was in council with his father and the advisors when cheers came from outside. Saul raised his head in irritation. "What is going on out there?"

The city was in an uproar of excitement. "David!" The people shouted. *"David!"*

Saul's face darkened for a moment, and then he rose. "Your friend returns. Go and greet him." He looked at the others. "We will follow."

Jonathan ran. He laughed when he saw David, for no one had to ask if his quest had been successful. A bloody sack was in his hand. "You did it!"

"*Two* hundred." David held up the sack.

"May the Lord be with you every day of your life! Michal will be dancing when she hears the news." Most likely she already had. His sister would be blessed with a husband who could protect her. He saw his father come outside. "Come, David! The king waits!"

Jonathan brought his friend to Saul. "Two hundred foreskins, Father. Twice what you asked for!"

David bowed low and held the sack out to the king. "The bride price for your daughter, my king."

A muscle twitched below Saul's right eye, and then he smiled broadly, held his arms wide. "My son!"

As the king engulfed David in his arms, the people went wild with joy.

+   +   +

Preparations were quickly made for the wedding. As
David's best friend, Jonathan took care of overseeing the
details. There would be food for thousands and wine to
wash it down. The king was glum, but the prince spared
no expense. After all, the daughter of the king was marrying Israel's champion. The tribes of Benjamin and Judah
would become allies forever.

No one tried to convince Jonathan otherwise.

Jonathan put the groom's crown on David's head.
"You're ready." He put his hand firmly on David's shoulder. "Stop shaking."

David's forehead was beaded with moisture. "I have
followed the Law since my youth, Jonathan, but I feel ill
prepared for marriage." He raised his brows.

"Michal is not an enemy, my friend. And she loves
you."

David blushed. "We'll see how she feels about me
tomorrow morning."

Chuckling, Jonathan gave him a shove toward the door.

Michal had never looked more beautiful or joyful than
when she stood beneath the canopy with David. Her dark
eyes glowed as she looked at him. When David took her
hand, a pulse beat in her throat. People smiled and whispered among themselves.

Representatives from all the tribes came to the wedding,
Judah in full force. Campfires dotted the landscape around
Gibeah. The sound of harps and tambourines drifted
through the night, along with the people's laughter.

King Saul announced his gift at the banquet: a house
near the king. David was stunned and grateful by such a

show of generosity, and praised the king for it. Saul raised his goblet of wine. The people sang and danced.

Jonathan leaned close. "The people are pleased, Father."

King Saul sipped, watching the festivities over the rim of his cup. "Let us hope we have not sown the seeds of our own destruction!"

FOUR

JONATHAN found it difficult to concentrate on Michal's litany of complaints, having just come from a tense meeting with his father. The next time his sister requested a visit with him, perhaps he should refuse.

Michal might adore David, but she whined endlessly about the burdens of David's responsibilities. Jonathan was thankful not to have a wife. How hard it must be for David to concentrate on Philistine threats when the most immediate threat was a tantrum in his own home.

"I wish he wasn't Israel's champion. If he was an ordinary soldier, I'd be delighted," she grumbled.

Jonathan knew better.

"At least then he could stay home a year! No one would miss him!"

Lounging, Jonathan considered her. "You and David have had a month without interruption." Long enough to conceive a child. "Now, the king wants him back on duty. Complaining won't alter the needs of the nation, Michal."

"Every time a village is raided, it's my husband who has to go out again. Why can't you be the one to go all the time? You have no wife."

Jonathan would like nothing better, but the king often sent him on other errands, especially to speak for unity among the tribes. "You should be proud of David."

"I am proud. But . . ."

Here it comes.

"You know the Law better than anyone, Jonathan. Doesn't it say when a man takes a new wife, he isn't to go off with the army or be charged with *any* duty other than to give happiness to her?"

He smiled cynically. "I'm delighted you're taking an interest in the Law, though you have dubious motives. You cannot choose one Law and ignore all the rest."

Her eyes blazed. "I'm not happy! It says I'm to have my husband long enough to be happy."

And how long would that take? "You're a daughter of the king of Israel. Shouldn't you be thinking of what is best for our people?"

Chin tipping, she looked away. "It's not fair!"

"Is it fair that the Philistines strip the poor of their sustenance? Of all our commanders, David has the most success against our enemies. The king is wise to use him."

"Or would you rather have the war come to our doorstep?" David spoke from the doorway.

Michal glanced up, blushing. Embarrassed, she grew angry. "You would think my father wanted you dead the number of times he sends you out!"

Jonathan rose in anger. "Only a fool speaks such nonsense!"

"A fool?" She glared up at him. "It's true, Jonathan! The only fool around here is—"

"Be quiet!" David said.

"You spend more time with my brother than you do with me!"

Red-faced, David came to her, drew her up, and led her aside. He kept his voice low as he leaned close and spoke to her. Any other man would have slapped her. Jonathan was pleased that his friend was forgiving. Hopefully, Michal would appreciate her husband's patience and compassion. Her shoulders slumped. She bowed her head. She sniffled and wiped her eyes. He tipped her chin, kissed her cheek, and spoke again, and she left the room.

David faced Jonathan, clearly mortified by his wife's behavior. "My servant will see her home. I'm sorry, Jonathan. She doesn't mean the things she says."

"Why are you apologizing? My sister is the one who can't hold her tongue."

"She's my wife, Jonathan."

"A rebuke?"

David looked uncomfortable.

"Sit. Relax." Jonathan smiled. "It speaks well of you that you are protective of your wife. She is right about the Law, my friend. It does call for a bridegroom's year at home to make a woman happy, and the way to do that is to fill her with child." Unfortunately, the king had no intention of following that particular law. He feared the Philistines more than God.

"I'm trying."

Jonathan laughed. He rose and slapped David's back. "Come, my friend. Let's look over the maps." They spent the next few hours in deliberation, discussing tactics and making plans. A servant came with refreshments.

David tore a piece of bread and dipped it in his wine. "Why haven't you taken a wife, Jonathan?"

From what Jonathan had seen of David and Michal's turbulent relationship, he was not eager to add a woman to his household. "I have no time for a wife."

"You will need an heir. And a woman gives comfort to a man."

Was Michal a comfort to David? Physically perhaps, but what about a man's other needs? Peace and quiet, a place to rest from trouble. "A contentious woman is worse than a bleating goat outside the window."

"You like women."

Jonathan grinned. "Ah, but they do not dance and sing around me as they do you."

"They dance and sing around me because I am one of them, a common man, a shepherd, youngest of my father's sons. But you, Jonathan. You stand as tall as your father, and from the gossip I hear, the women find you even more handsome. And you are the prince, heir to the throne of Israel. They wait at the gates in hope you will look at them, and when you do, they blush. You could have any woman you want, my friend."

Jonathan knew women liked him. And he liked women. "There is a time for all things, David. Right now, Israel is my beloved. The people are my wife. Perhaps when we have peace—"

"It may be years before we have peace. The Lord said it is not good for a man to be alone."

Jonathan sometimes longed for the comfort of home and family, but other matters must take precedence. "When a man loves a woman, his heart is divided. Remember how Adam sought to please Eve when she offered him the apple? He knew the Lord forbade it and took the fruit anyway." He shook his head. "No. Israel holds my heart. When God's enemies are driven from our land, then I will take a wife." He grinned. "And I will stay at home for a full year to make her happy."

+   +   +

They met each day, going out into the field for a few hours of practice with their weapons. Jonathan cherished the time with his friend and knew David felt the same. Out in the open, beyond the gates and houses, they could talk as they shot arrows and threw spears while their young servants retrieved them.

"Even with your success, we're still far from winning the war." Jonathan sent his arrow winging to the target. "The Philistines keep coming like waves from the sea. We have to stem the tide."

"And how do we do that?" David hurled his spear farther than the last time and hit just off center.

"Philistine weaponry is far superior to ours."

"We strip the dead of their weapons."

"That's not enough." Jonathan shook his head. "When those weapons are damaged, we don't know how to repair them. We can't forge swords like theirs. And their spear tips and arrows go through bronze." He took a handful of arrows from Ebenezer and dropped them into the quiver on his back.

"What's your idea?" David hurled another spear.

"Find men willing to go to Gath."

"And trade for the secret?" David asked.

Jonathan shot another arrow straight to the target. "The Philistines are too shrewd. They won't share their knowledge easily. Someone would have to go and gain their trust in order to learn how to make their weapons."

"A pity they know I'm the one who killed Goliath."

"You'd be the last one they'd welcome."

"What about those men who lived among them before Micmash? They've returned to the ranks of Israel, but maybe a few of them would agree to go back and—"

"I don't think they'd be trusted either. Would you trust a man whose loyalty was swayed whichever way the battle went? I don't trust them." Jonathan shot another arrow straight and true. "Move the target back! It's too easy." He turned to David. "The Lord could destroy all our enemies with one breath, David, but He told *us* to clear the land. I believe He did that to test our loyalty to Him. Would we do as He said? Our forefathers did for a generation and then lost sight of the goal—and of God."

The servant called out that the target was ready, and Jonathan turned and shot his arrow.

"Dead center!" the boy shouted and gave a whoop.

"Move it back again!" Jonathan raised his bow. "We must teach the people to pray and then fight, but it would also help if we had stronger swords!"

✦   ✦   ✦

Jonathan and David went out together to hunt Philistine raiders. Camped beneath the stars, David picked at the strings of his harp, playing a song of celebration over their enemies. "Why is it you never sing, Jonathan?"

Jonathan smirked. "God gives each of us gifts, my friend. Singing isn't one the Lord saw fit to give me."

"Every man can sing. Sing with me, Jonathan!" Some of the men joined him in urging the prince to give it a try.

Laughing, Jonathan decided there was only one way to convince them. David's eyes flickered, but he said nothing. The other men sang louder, some grinning. When the song was over, Jonathan lay back and put his arms behind his head.

David continued to play his harp, trying out new chords and fingerings.

"The king will like that," Jonathan said.

When they returned to Gibeah and dined with the

king, Saul ordered David to sing for him. "Sing a new song."

The chamber filled with beautiful music as David strummed gently and plucked at the instrument. Only he could bring sounds of such sweetness and words of grace. But when David started to sing, Jonathan grinned.

"Make a joyful noise—" David grinned back at him before continuing.

✦   ✦   ✦

After several weeks of chasing Philistines and strengthening outposts, Jonathan returned to Gibeah to learn that David had routed another band of raiders and sent them running for their lives.

His father summoned him. Jonathan expected to find the king well pleased. Instead, Saul paced, livid, while his advisors stood about watching uneasily. What had caused the foul mood this time? Nothing but good news had come in from all fronts, the most glorious from David's.

Abner closed the door behind Jonathan. "We are all here, my lord."

Saul turned. "I want David killed."

Jonathan froze, staring. What madness was this?

"This Judean threatens my rule! Did you hear the people shouting his name yesterday when he approached the gates of *my* city?"

Jonathan shook his head, unable to understand his father's fury. "Because he sent the enemy running."

"You understand nothing! You call my enemy *your friend*!"

Heat surged into Jonathan's face, his heart bounding

in alarm and anger. "David is your friend as well, my lord. And your son, by marriage to Michal!"

Saul turned away from him. "If we allow this shepherd to continue to gain power, he will assassinate me and take the crown for himself."

Jonathan looked at the others in the room. Would no one speak sense to the king? Abner returned his gaze, nodding. "David could become a threat."

"Have you ever seen evidence of an insurrection?"

"By the time there is evidence, I'll be dead!" Saul raged.

Jonathan extended his hands toward his father. "You couldn't be more wrong about David. He has no ambitions other than to serve you."

"He steals the people's affection!"

"The people love you! They cry out your name as well as David's, Father."

"Not as loudly. Not as long."

Jonathan glared at the others. Would they let suspicion grow in Saul because they were afraid to speak the truth? David was Saul's greatest ally! "Are the Philistines not enemies enough for you? We need not invent one in our midst!"

Abner spoke for the rest. "An enemy in our midst can do the most damage."

Jonathan knew he would have to find a way to speak to his father alone, for these men would say anything to please the king. They were too influenced by Saul's fears and unwittingly fanned the fire of his wounded pride by agreeing with him.

But until he could draw Saul away from these men, Jonathan had to make certain David was removed from harm's way. He found David in a meeting with his officers. "We must talk. Now."

David led him into another room. "What is it, Jonathan? What's wrong?"

"My father is looking for a chance to kill you."

David paled. "Why?"

"He's having one of his spells. You've seen it before. It will pass."

"I pray that you're right!"

"Tomorrow morning, you must find a hiding place out in the fields." Jonathan took his arm and told him where to go. "I'll ask my father to go out there with me, and I'll talk to him about you. Then I'll tell you everything I can find out. But you must take no chances, my friend. Some of the king's advisors see enemies where there are none."

✦   ✦   ✦

Jonathan joined his father before the morning meal.

Saul looked exhausted and drawn, dark shadows beneath his eyes. When he reached for his goblet of wine, his hand trembled.

"You did not sleep well." And no wonder if all the king could think about was the rise of an adversary. Jonathan intended to clear his father's mind of those fears.

Saul scowled. "How could I sleep with my kingdom in jeopardy?"

Placing the bowl of honey close, Jonathan tore off a hunk of bread and offered it to his father. Saul took it, still frowning, pensive. Men stood in the antechamber, waiting for an audience with the king. Jonathan needed to get his father away from the palace and out into the open air for a while. "Remember how we cleared fields together, Father?"

Saul made a soft sound, gazing off toward the windows.

"The fields are almost ready for reapers. The Lord has blessed us with a good harvest this year." He offered his father dates. "It's been days since you left the palace." And the company of his advisors. "You've worked hard for your people, Father. Surely you are allowed a walk in the fields of the Lord."

Rising, Saul glowered at the men approaching. "Go away."

Servants backed away.

Jonathan hadn't expected it to be so easy.

They walked half the morning and sat beneath one of the olive trees.

Saul sighed. "I miss this."

"I would speak to you of your command yesterday, Father."

"Which one?"

"The one you issued to kill David."

Saul turned his head and looked at him. "Is that why you brought me out here?"

"Yes. And no."

"Which do you mean?"

"I see how burdened you are. Not a week goes by that we must send men out to protect our land from raiders. And the tribes constantly bicker among themselves over petty things. But remember, they all assemble at your command, my lord." He looked into his father's eyes. "You know I love you. You know I honor you. Do you trust me?"

"Yes."

"The king must not sin against his servant David. He's never done anything to harm you. He has always helped you in any way he could. Have you forgotten about the time he risked his life to kill the Philistine giant and how the Lord brought a great victory to all Israel as a result? You were certainly happy about it then."

Saul's shoulders slumped. "No. I will never forget it."

"Why should you murder an innocent man like David? There is no reason for it at all!" He spoke gently, wanting to remind his father of what was right, hoping to turn his mind from the advice of cowards. "If there is any man in the kingdom you can trust more than me, it is your son-in-law David."

Saul grimaced as if in pain. "When I hear what he accomplishes—" He shook his head.

"Everything David has accomplished is for the Lord's glory and yours, Father. He is your faithful servant." Jonathan wanted to speak more of David's achievements, but worried they would distress rather than comfort his father. "With all due respect for your advisors, Father, they are frightened men. Let wisdom rather than fear reign over Israel."

Leaning his head back against the gnarled trunk of the olive tree, Saul closed his eyes and sighed.

Jonathan remained silent. He did not want to press his father as other men did. He looked out over the fields and then up at the blue heavens.

"You are my eldest son, Jonathan, the first show of my strength as a man. The people hold you in high regard. When I die, the crown will pass to you."

"God willing."

When Saul glanced at him, Jonathan felt his heart fillip.

He had not meant to remind his father of what Samuel had said.

"I wonder what God was thinking when He chose me to be king."

Jonathan relaxed. "That you were the man the people wanted."

"Yes." Such bleakness. "The people wanted me. Once."

"They still do. You need not worry, Father." *Lord, let him hear my words.* "The people will always love a king who reigns with wisdom and honor."

"Their love is like the wind, Jonathan, blowing east one day and west the next."

"Then you must steady them with a calm spirit."

"I'm tired."

"Rest a while now. I'll keep watch."

And Saul did. He slept several hours while Jonathan remained with him in the olive grove. When servants came to check on the king, Jonathan motioned them away. Every man needed to rest, especially a king.

When his father awakened, he smiled. "I dreamed I was a farmer again."

"The Lord has called you to another purpose."

His father started to rise. Jonathan got to his feet and extended his hand. Saul clasped it and pulled himself up. "You're not a boy anymore." He smiled slightly. "I keep forgetting." He put his hand on Jonathan's shoulder. "As surely as the Lord lives, David will not be killed."

Jonathan bowed low. "May the Lord reward your wisdom, Father."

"We can hope so." Saul saw his servants coming. "I have things to do." He walked toward them.

Jonathan went out farther into the fields. "David!"

"I am here." David came out of hiding and walked toward him. It hurt Jonathan to see his friend so tentative. He smiled when he came closer. "I can see by your face that you believe things went well with the king."

Jonathan put his arm around his friend's shoulders. "There is no need for you to look uncertain, my friend." He released him. "Come. I will take you to him. You will see for yourself that things will be as they were before. Bring your harp."

✦   ✦   ✦

Things were indeed better between the king and his champion. Jonathan saw the peace David brought the king with his songs of deliverance. For a time, the Philistines were quiet and Gibeah basked in the sun. Jonathan would look back on those days as the most peaceful he had known. He and David spent long hours together, poring over the Law, discussing it. No one else among their friends and relatives shared their fascination.

"Until I faced Goliath, my brothers thought I was fit only to watch sheep. No matter what I said, they accused me of something. That day in the valley of Elah, Eliab said I was conceited and wicked for speaking out."

"They didn't know you very well."

"I wonder if they ever will." An expression flickered across David's face and was gone, a grimness Jonathan had not seen before.

Jonathan lifted a jug of fresh water and filled his goblet. "How wonderful and pleasant it would be if all brothers could live together in harmony!" He drank deeply and set his cup aside. "That's my one dream, David, the work I believe God intends for me. To help my father bring the tribes together. We cannot be scattered flocks bleating at one another. If we are to conquer our enemies, we must unite with our brothers and stand firm behind God's anointed king. We must remember our covenant with the Lord, for that covenant with God is what will hold us together."

"You are blessed." David smiled. "You have a copy of the Law with you wherever you go."

If only his father the king had made a copy of the Law for himself. If only Saul had taken the command seriously, perhaps he would not have sinned. And if his father had studied the Law, he would know that the Lord was slow to anger and quick to forgive.

"However many days God gives me upon this earth, David, it will not be enough to know all that He has for us in the Law. It is new every morning that I read it. I wish the Lord in His mercy would write it upon our hearts, for it seems to me, our minds are not able to absorb the lengths and depths of the love God has for us as His chosen people."

✦   ✦   ✦

Yet again, Saul sent David out to fight, and he struck the Philistines with such force that they fled before him. He returned in triumph and the city and countryside celebrated. The king and his officers, David and Jonathan among them, feasted in the palace. Outside, warriors sang songs of victory written by David.

Many of the officers drank heavily. "Sing us a song, David!"

"Yes! Sing us a song!"

David looked at King Saul.

Jonathan felt the air growing thinner. He waited for his

father to speak, wondering why he sat with his back against the wall, a spear in his hand, daydreaming. "Father?"

"Yes—" Saul waved his hand—"sing."

David's servant brought him the harp. As the chamber was filled with his playing, one of the advisors remarked, "He casts spells with his music."

Saul's gaze shifted.

Jonathan glared at the man. "I believe you have duties elsewhere." The advisor glanced at the king, but Saul said nothing. Jonathan did not take his gaze from the man until he excused himself, rose, and left the room.

Relaxing back onto the cushions, Jonathan listened to David singing:

> *"Give to the Lord the glory He deserves!*
> *Bring your offering and come into His courts.*
> *Worship the Lord in all His holy splendor.*
> *Let all the earth tremble before Him."*

Men clapped when he plucked the last chords. The king smiled and nodded.

A servant bent close to Jonathan. "Your mother requests your presence, my lord prince."

Surprised, Jonathan asked his father's permission to leave. It was not his mother's custom to ask for him. "Go." Saul barely glanced at him, his gaze still fixed upon David as he began to play another song.

Jonathan's mother had lavish quarters now, and servants to wait upon her every need. When he entered, a pretty servant girl bowed before him and ushered him into his mother's chamber.

She was reclining on a couch, cheeks sallow. "I am sorry to take you away from your celebration, my son."

"You're ill," Jonathan said, alarmed. "Why wasn't I told?"

"I'm not so ill that anyone should know. Bring my son a cushion, Rachel."

Jonathan sat and took his mother's hand. "What do the physicians say?"

His mother patted his hand as if he were a child. "The physicians know nothing. I just need rest. Jonathan, I would like you to meet Rachel, daughter of my second cousin. Her father is a scribe."

Jonathan glanced at the blushing girl. She was very pretty.

His mother nodded and the girl slipped from the room. "She's pretty, don't you think? And she comes from a good family." When his mother struggled to sit up, Jonathan got up to help her. "I'm comfortable now. Sit." She smiled. "Rachel's father knows Samuel."

"You asked to see me. Why?"

"I should think it's obvious." She pressed her lips together. "You should marry, my son, and soon."

"This is not the time."

"What better time is there? You are far older than your father was when we married."

"Mother, my responsibilities leave me no time for—"

"David is married. You pressed for that match, didn't you? And he's younger than you are."

Amused, Jonathan shook his head. "I suppose every mother wants her children settled." He leaned toward her, wanting her to rest and not worry. "David's marriage to Michal strengthens the bond between our tribe and Judah,

Mother. And besides, what better man could there be for your daughter than Israel's champion?"

Her eyes darkened. "You are Israel's champion, my son. You were scarcely older than David when you routed the Philistines at Micmash. Though many years have passed since then, the people have not forgotton. There are equally good reasons for you to marry, Jonathan."

He felt the tremor in her hand. "Why are you pressing this, Mother?"

Her eyes welled with tears. "Because I don't know from one battle to the next if my son will be killed." Her voice broke. "Is it too much to ask that I hold a grandchild in my arms?"

"Michal and David—"

"No!"

He frowned, troubled by her vehemence.

She sat up and leaned toward him. "Marry and have sons of your own, Jonathan. You and your brothers must have sons to build up Saul's house."

"Why are you so adamant now?"

"We must increase in numbers."

"You have more faith in me than I have in myself if you think I can increase the population—"

"It's not a laughing matter."

He sighed. "No. But it's not the right time either."

"I—"

"No, Mother."

"If it pleases the king for you to marry . . ."

"If it were on his mind, he would have suggested it himself. And if he does now, I'll tell him his wife has put him up to it." Jonathan kissed her cheek and rose. "You and David—"

Her head came up. "What about David?"

"He agrees with you. He told me the Scriptures say it is not good for a man to be alone, that he should have a wife." He tilted his head at her expression. "Why does that surprise you?"

"If you won't listen to your mother, perhaps you should listen to your friend."

"Later, perhaps."

✦ ✦ ✦

Jonathan awakened abruptly from a sound sleep and heard Michal's voice. "I don't care if he's asleep! I must see my brother! *Now*!"

Jonathan sat up and rubbed his face. He had slept fitfully, awakened by strange dreams. Violence in the city. Philistines on the rampage. The walls breeched. Twice he had lunged up, grabbed his sword, and gone to the window, only to find Gibeah quiet.

His servant stood in the doorway. "My lord, I'm sorry to awaken you. Your sister—"

"I heard her. Tell her I will be with her in a moment." He stripped off his tunic, splashed water on his face, and toweled dry. Donning a fresh tunic and robe, he went out to her.

Michal paced, her face splotched from crying, her eyes wild. "Finally!"

She reminded him of their father in one of his moods. "What's going on?" It was then he noticed the bruise on her cheek.

"Father hit me! You have to speak with him. He was so angry I thought he would kill me!" She sobbed. "He's out of his mind! You have to help me!"

He felt a sudden fear. "Where's David?"

"Gone!"

He took her hands and made her sit. "Gone where, Michal?"

"I don't know where. Running for his life. He's gone! And I'm left to face the king!" She cried like a frightened child and shrieked at him, "It's all your fault, Jonathan!"

"How is it my fault?"

"My husband would still be home in bed with me if you'd stayed at the feast! Why did you leave?"

"Mother asked for me."

She gulped air and used her shawl to wipe her eyes and nose. "She's dying of a broken heart because Father took that girl Rizpah to his bed. He doesn't care about her any-more."

Jonathan hadn't been pleased when he heard about it. "Mother is still his queen, Michal, and the mother of his children."

She rose, frustrated. "I didn't come to talk about her problems. After you left the celebration the evil spirit came upon Father again. You know how he is when that happens."

All too well.

"He was sitting with his spear in his hand."

A kingly pose after a great victory.

"One minute he seemed fine, and the next, he was hurling his spear at David! He drove it into the wall! David eluded him and came home. He thought Father's advisors would calm him down, but when I heard what had happened I knew Father was determined to kill my husband. I told David if he didn't leave Gibeah, he would be dead before morning. And I was

right! He wasn't gone more than a few minutes when
Father's men came. I told them David was ill. So they
went back to the king, but Father sent them again
with orders to bring David, sick or not! Aren't you
going to ask how David got away?" She clenched her
hands. "I let him down from the window. Then I took
one of my idols and laid it in our bed. I covered it
with a garment and put some goat's hair on its head."
She laughed wildly. "Wasn't that clever of me?
Wasn't it?"

"Yes." Jonathan was revolted at the thought of his
sister's having idols in the house.

"And then Father's men came again. When they found
David wasn't there, they brought *me* to the king instead.
And Father accused me of deceiving him and sending his
enemy away so that he could escape. His *enemy*! Oh, Jonathan, I thought he was going to have me executed for
treason!"

Jonathan forced himself to speak calmly. "He would not
kill his own daughter, Michal."

She grew angry. "You didn't see his face. You didn't
look into his eyes. I told him David threatened to kill me
if I didn't help him get away."

Jonathan drew back and stared.

"Why are you looking at me like that?"

"What sort of wife betrays her husband with such a lie?
David wouldn't hurt a hair on your head!"

"Father was ready to lop it off!"

"How you talk! You're here, Michal. Alive and well. No
guards with you. Whatever storm you imagined has probably already passed."

She flew to her feet, her face contorted with anger.

"You're wrong! Sometimes I wonder if you even know our father. You're so determined to see the good in everyone."

"And you're even quicker to seek faults in everyone."

Her neck stiffened. "Maybe you're wrong about David, too. Did that ever occur to you? Your fine friend didn't stay around to protect his wife, did he? He left without a second thought. Did he stop to think what would happen to me?"

"You took care of yourself, didn't you?"

"I hate you! I hate you almost as much as I hate—"

Jonathan gave her a hard shake. "Lower your voice!"

Michal sagged, weeping, her head resting against his chest. "What am I going to do without him? I love him! I don't want to be a widow."

Jonathan thought of David running for his life. "Where was he going?"

She pushed away. "How would I know? To his family, I suppose. I don't remember. Bethlehem." She wilted onto a cushion and covered her face, her shoulders shaking with sobs. "Will you speak to Father for me? Please, Jonathan. I'm afraid of what he'll do."

+ + +

Jonathan wondered if his sister had exaggerated everything, for the king was in a good mood the next day. "You retired early last night, my son. Were you unwell?"

"Mother summoned me. Is everything all right?"

"Yes! Of course. Why wouldn't it be?"

"Michal came to my house last night."

Saul scowled. "Your sister invents trouble. Speak no more of her." He waved his hand, as though to slap the subject away. "What of your mother? Why did she call you away from the celebration?"

He leaned close and spoke softly so the advisors would not hear. "She thinks it's time I marry."

"Does she?" Saul's brows rose. He considered the thought and then nodded. "Not a bad idea. We should find you a suitable young woman."

Jonathan knew what *suitable* would mean to his father: a bride to bring an alliance. "She must be from the tribe of Benjamin, Father. As the Law requires."

Saul's expression changed. "It will have to wait." He put his arm around Jonathan's shoulder. "The Philistines plundered another village." They reviewed the reports together.

Jonathan pointed out his strategies. "With your permission, I'll take David with me."

The king looked thunderous. "And share the glory?" He shook his head. "Not this time."

"It is not glory I seek, Father, but an end to this war. We can't give the Philistines a single village or field. We must drive them out of the land or we will never have peace."

"Call out your men and go!" Saul turned his back. "I have other plans for David."

+   +   +

Weeks passed with some minor skirmishes, but Jonathan didn't find the multitude of Philistines reported. Something was wrong.

He returned to Gibeah and learned that his father had gone to Ramah. "Did Samuel call for him?"

"No, my lord. The king sent men to Naioth in Ramah to summon David, but he was no longer with Samuel."

David had been with Samuel?

"Twice more, the king sent men, but the Spirit of the Lord came upon them and they prophesied in Samuel's presence. So the king went himself. And then the Spirit of the Lord came upon him as well and he prophesied."

Strange happenings indeed, but Jonathan grasped hope. Perhaps his father had repented!

Let it be so, Lord! Let it be so!

✦   ✦   ✦

Jonathan rose early to read the Law, then went out to practice with his bow. David came out of the rocks and called to him. Jonathan ran to meet him.

"What have I done, Jonathan? What is my crime?"

Jonathan remembered Michal's visit in the night. Perhaps he had dismissed her too quickly. "What are you talking about?"

"How have I offended your father that he is so determined to kill me?"

"That's not true!" Jonathan grasped his arms. "You're not going to die!"

"The king tried to pin me to the wall with his spear. If not for Michal, I'd be dead. I hid at the stone pile. I could think of nothing else to do but go to Samuel and ask his help. The king sent three parties of men after me and then came himself."

"And made peace with Samuel. I heard. All is well. He prophesied. He has turned back to the Lord!" The king had not seen Samuel since the debacle at Gilgal. His father had loathed the very mention of Samuel's name. All that must have changed!

David shook his head, anguished. "I'm running for my

life, Jonathan. You're the only one I can trust, the only hope I have of finding out why the king is so determined to kill me!"

Jonathan felt how David trembled from exhaustion and fear. Was everyone going mad? "Rest. Here. Eat some grain." He took the pouch from his belt. "Drink." He gave him the skin of water. "All this is a misunderstanding. Look, my father always tells me everything he's going to do, even the little things. I know my father wouldn't hide something like this from me. It just isn't so! You know how he is sometimes. His moods pass. A spear thrown in a fit of temper doesn't mean the king is plotting to murder you. Why would he do such a thing? Your victories rally the armies of God." But a niggling worry took hold of him even as he spoke. *Let it not be so, Lord.* "No! It's not true!" He refused to believe it.

"Jonathan, your father knows perfectly well about our friendship, so he has said to himself, 'I won't tell Jonathan—why should I hurt him?' But I swear to you that I am only a step away from death! I swear it by the Lord and by your own soul!"

David's fear was real, and he must be proven wrong. "Tell me what I can do to help you."

David looked around, a hunted look on his face. "Look, tomorrow we celebrate the new moon festival. I've always eaten with the king on this occasion, but tomorrow I'll hide in the field and stay there until the evening of the third day. If your father asks where I am, tell him I asked permission to go home to Bethlehem for an annual family sacrifice. If he says, 'Fine!' you will know all is well. But if he is angry and loses his temper, you will know he is determined to kill me." His voice broke with pent-up emotion. "Show me this loyalty as my sworn friend—for we made a solemn pact before the Lord—or kill me yourself if I have sinned against your father. But please don't betray me to him!"

"Never!" Jonathan exclaimed. "You know that if I had the slightest notion my father was planning to kill you, I would tell you at once." Surely David was wrong. Surely Michal had exaggerated. His father had seemed himself the next morning he spoke with him.

But why did he send me away?

And the reports were incorrect. All that wasted time.

Or was it?

"How will I know whether or not your father is angry?"

"Come out to the field with me."

They walked across the hills together. They had spent many hours out here practicing with bow and spear, running races.

"Do you believe me, Jonathan?"

"I don't know what to believe." He turned to David. "But I can tell you this. I promise by the Lord, the God of Israel, that by this time tomorrow, or the next day at the latest, I will talk to my father and let you know at once how he feels about you. If he speaks favorably about you, I will let you know. But if he is angry and wants you killed, may the Lord strike me and even kill me if I don't warn you so you can escape and live." He clasped David's hand. "May the Lord be with you as He used to be with my father."

Jonathan knew David had no ambitions to take the throne, but he was not so certain about David's relatives. What if they were as ambitious for David as Kish and

Abner had been for Saul? David's relatives—Joab, Abishai, and Asahel—were known to be cunning warriors. And they would urge David to follow the ways of the surrounding nations.

"And may you treat me with the faithful love of the Lord as long as I live. But if I die, treat my family with this faithful love, even when the Lord destroys all your enemies from the face of the earth."

"I will never break my covenant with you, Jonathan. I am your friend until my last breath!"

"And I yours." Jonathan felt something else, something far bigger than he could understand, at play here. Only one thing did he hold tight. His father might suffer from fits of rage, but he was not David's enemy. However, there might be several enemies in the ranks of his father's advisors. Snakes coiled and ready to strike. "May the Lord destroy all your enemies, no matter who they are."

Jonathan tried to think of where the safest place would be for David to hide until he could set his mind at ease about Saul. "As you said, tomorrow we celebrate the new moon festival. You will be missed when your place at the table is empty." Jonathan would make certain the seating arrangements were unchanged. David was irreplaceable. "The day after tomorrow, toward evening, go to the place where you hid before, and wait there by the stone pile. I will come out and shoot three arrows to the side of the stone pile as though I were shooting at a target. Then I will send a boy to bring the arrows back. If you hear me tell him, 'They're on this side,' then you will know, as surely as the Lord lives, that all is well, and there is no trouble. But if I tell him, 'Go farther—the arrows are still

ahead of you,' then it will mean that you must leave immediately, for the Lord is sending you away."

David thanked him. They embraced and turned their
separate ways.

Michal's words came back to Jonathan, strident with
warning. Could he be mistaken about his friend? No. He
couldn't be wrong about David. He knew him as well as
he knew himself. But he could not forget about Samuel's
prophecy. God had torn the kingdom from Saul and given
it to another. And not long after that proclamation, Samuel
had gone to Bethlehem. Saul had sent men to question
him, and Samuel had said he had gone to sacrifice. But
why there? And now, with this trouble between his father
and David, his friend had run to Samuel.

*Is David the one, Lord? Or am I to be king after my
father?* If Samuel had anointed David in Bethlehem, it
would explain his father's wild behavior. But Samuel had
said he had gone to sacrifice. Would a prophet lie?

The tribe of Judah might still covet the crown.

Jonathan turned back. "David!" When his friend
turned, he called out to him. "And may the Lord make us
keep our promises to each other, for He has witnessed
them." As long as they were true friends, all might be
well, no matter what happened.

"Forever!" David raised his hand.

Jonathan smiled and waved. David's word was enough.
It was his bond.

✦   ✦   ✦

When the new moon festival came, Jonathan sat in his
usual place opposite his father. Saul held a spear in his
hand. Abner sat beside the king and they whispered

together several times. Both commanded a full view of the entire room and entrance, and their relatives sat in the best positions to guard Saul.

The king looked at David's empty seat. Irritation flickered, but he said nothing about his absence. Jonathan relaxed and ate. David's worries were unnecessary. Jonathan could hardly wait to tell him. Still, he should wait until tomorrow and see if the king said anything about David on the second day.

And the king did ask. "Why hasn't the son of Jesse been here for the meal either yesterday or today?" Something in his father's face made the sweat break out on the back of Jonathan's neck when his father raised the question.

No. David cannot be right. Michal exaggerated. Father would not plot murder. He could not!

The room fell silent. Jonathan looked around at his relatives. "David earnestly asked me if he could go to Bethlehem." He looked into his father's eyes. *Don't let it be true!* "He said, 'Please let me go, for we are having a family sacrifice. My brother demanded that I be there. So please let me get away to see my brothers.' That's why he isn't here at the king's table."

Saul's eyes went black with malevolence. "You stupid son of a whore!"

Shocked, Jonathan stared speechless. And then a rush of anger spilled into his blood. His mother, a whore?

"Do you think I don't know that you want him to be king in your place, shaming yourself and your mother?" Face florid, hands clenched white, Saul glared, a muscle twitching near his right eye.

It's true! Everything David said is true! God, help us all!

"As long as that son of Jesse is alive, you'll never be king."

"It is not *my* kingship that worries you."

"Now go and get him so I can kill him!"

Jonathan came to his feet. "But why should he be put to death? What has he done?"

Screaming in rage, Saul hurled the spear at Jonathan with all his might.

Jonathan barely avoided being pinned to the wall. Men scrambled. Servants fled. Relatives shouted. Stunned and furious, Jonathan rushed to the doorway. "Your struggle is not with David or me, Father. It is with the Lord our God!" He strode from the room, grinding his teeth in anger.

Storming into his house, he ordered the servants out, closed all the doors, and gave vent to his wrath. Holding his head, he screamed in frustration. *Am I becoming like my father? Lord, don't let me become a captive of fear!* He longed to leave Gibeah. He wanted to get as far away from Saul as he could. How could he have been so wrong? Was it possible to spend so much time with a man and not know what went on in his mind?

What do I do now? What is right?

He moved near the lamp and took the Law from beneath his tunic.

God, help me. What am I to do?

"Be holy as I am holy. . . ."

How, Lord? How could he get past words like *honor your father . . . ?*

How do I honor a man who plots murder, who grasps hold of power like a child holds on to a toy, who ignores the needs of his people to satisfy his own lusts for power and posses-

sions. What happened to the father I knew, the man who didn't want to be king?

"Show me the path, Lord! Help me!" His hands trembled as he read, for words he had loved to read now cut deep and made his soul bleed.

"Honor your father. . . ."

If he sided with David, he dishonored his father. If he sided with his father, he would sin against God. Honor. Truth.

I love them both!

His soul was in anguish.

You anointed my father king over Israel. But if You have chosen David now . . . which one do I serve, Lord?

Serve Me.

Tears dripped onto the parchment. He carefully dried them so they would not smudge the Word of the Lord. He rolled the scroll up, tucked it into its casing, and slipped it back inside his tunic. Gathering his bow and arrows, he opened the door.

Ebenezer waited just outside. "I will go with you."

"No." Jonathan strode out the door. As he walked through Gibeah, young boys ran alongside him. He chose one young boy from among them to accompany him. "The rest of you, go back inside the gates." He looked up at the watchman above him. The man gave a solemn nod.

They went out into the fields. "Start running, so you can find the arrows as I shoot them."

"Yes, my lord." The boy pranced with eagerness and then ran like a gazelle.

"The arrow is still ahead of you!" Jonathan called out. Had David heard him? Jonathan glanced back. What if his father had sent men to watch? They might capture David, and then his father would have innocent blood on his hands. "Hurry, hurry, don't wait."

The boy ran faster, gathering up the arrows and racing back.

Emotion filled Jonathan as he saw David's head rise a little from the rocks where he hid. Would David trust him? Why should he trust anyone in Saul's house? Jonathan slipped the arrows back into the quiver and handed it to the boy. He handed over his bow as well. "Go. Carry them back to town." David could see now that he had no weapons. Jonathan walked slowly toward the stone pile.

David came out and dropped to his knees, bowing down three times with his face to the ground.

Jonathan's throat closed. "Get up, David. I am not the king." Jonathan embraced him. They kissed as brothers. Jonathan wept. How long before they saw one another again? before they could sit by lamplight and read the Law together?

"I know the truth now, David. God will help us both. It is not right that this has happened to you, but the Lord will bring good from it. I am convinced of that."

David cried. "I can't go to my wife. I can't go home or Saul might think everyone in my family is his enemy. I can't go to Samuel without risking his life. Where am I to go, Jonathan?"

Tears ran down Jonathan's cheeks. "I don't know, David. All I know is this: The Lord will not abandon you. Trust in the Lord!"

David sobbed.

Jonathan looked back toward Gibeah. There was no time. His father's men might come at any minute.

What did the future hold?

Jonathan gripped David's arms and gave him a gentle shake. "Go in peace, for we have sworn loyalty to each other in the Lord's name. The Lord is the witness of a bond between us and our children forever."

David looked bereft. His mouth worked, but no words came.

Jonathan fought against the shame that filled him. How could his father hate David? How could he not see the goodness in him, the desire to serve the Lord with gladness and fight beside his king? Did any man in Israel love the Lord as David did? Sorrow filled him. *"Go!"* He gave him a shove. "Go quickly, my friend, and may God go with you!"

Still weeping, David ran.

Throat tight, tears streaming, Jonathan looked up. He raised his hands in the air. No words came. He didn't know what to pray. He just stood, feet spread, in the middle of the fields of the Lord, and silently surrendered to whatever God would do.

FIVE

SAUL had Jonathan brought to him, the prince fully expecting to be executed for treason. Refusing to bow his head, he stood before his father and waited.

What could he say? The king would not listen to the truth. *My life is in your hands, Lord. Do what You will.*

"I know of your covenant with David! You incited him to lie in wait for me!"

"Everyone knows of my friendship with David. They also know he has never lain in wait for you, nor have I betrayed you. He is your strongest ally, and your son by marriage."

"You are my son! You owe me loyalty!"

"And you have it! Who among your sycophants will tell you the truth, whether you want to hear it or not?" Jonathan was so angry he trembled.

Saul's eyes flickered. He turned away. He paced and then sat. "I was not myself when I threw the spear. Surely, you must know I would not kill you."

Jonathan didn't know whether to believe him or not. "It would appear I don't know anything anymore." Least of all the heart of his father.

+   +   +

Saul kept Jonathan close, including him in council meetings and when he listened to the people's cases beneath the tamarisk tree. Reports began to come in: David's parents now lived in Moab under the protection of its king. David had gone to Gath. At the news, Jonathan's heart

leapt. Could David fool King Achish into believing he
had turned his back on Israel?

"Do you see how David betrays me? He runs to our
enemy!"

Abner smiled grimly. "King Achish will execute him.
Goliath was not just Philistia's champion, but Gath's
favorite son."

Saul waved a parchment and threw it down. "He pre-
tends he is mad. They won't touch him for fear he is possessed by one of their gods."

Jonathan lowered his head so that neither his father nor
Abner would see how excited he was. If David was hiding
in Gath as the reports said, he was there for a reason other
than to wait out Saul's wrath.

He would find out how to forge iron weapons!

✦　✦　✦

Months passed and all was quiet. Jonathan attended his
father and offered sound advice when asked. Saul loosened his hold and gave Jonathan more freedom. Jonathan
continued to study the Law, while keeping abreast of
what was happening through Ebenezer, now a trusted
officer in the court.

One day Ebenezer came to Jonathan. "Your father is in
a rage, my lord. David is no longer in Gath. One of your
father's men saw David with Ahimelech, the leading priest
in Nob. The king prepares to leave within the hour with a
contingent of warriors."

Knowing anything he might say could fan his father's
anger, Jonathan ran to Abner. "You must dissuade the
king from this venture. Nothing good can come of it!"

Abner strapped on his sword. "Your friend may not be

as loyal as you believe. Every man has his ambitions. Did
you hear of Doeg's report?"

"Will you trust Doeg? an Edomite? You know what
they are like. The man is a troublemaker who would say
anything to find favor with the king."

"The king will be waiting."

"David will never raise his hand against the king!"

"How can you be so sure?"

"Because I know him! And so does the nation!"

"Your father is the king!"

"No one knows that better than David, or has shown
the king more honor and loyalty. I didn't go down into
that valley to fight Goliath. Nor did you. And yet David
went to Gath. Why, do you suppose? To learn how to
make iron weapons!"

Abner looked uncertain. "If that's so, why didn't he
come to Saul?"

"And be speared before he could open his mouth?"

"I must go."

"You would do King Saul and our people more good
if you told him the truth rather than follow like a
sheep!"

Abner turned, his face livid. "Perhaps you should
rethink your alliances, Jonathan. If Saul falls, so will
you! David may be your friend, but there are those in
Judah who would gladly see you dead if it placed David
on the throne!" He headed out the door.

"Abner!" Jonathan went to him. "I know of your loy-
alty and fierce heart. But remember, whatever you do,
God is watching. And God will judge your actions.
Remember that when you are in Nob."

✦   ✦   ✦

Each time a messenger entered the city, Jonathan dreaded the news. He prayed that David had escaped; he didn't want to hear of his friend's death. He prayed that his father would repent and turn back from Nob, not wanting to hear that his father had insulted Ahimelech or any other priest in Nob. The people seemed to feel the tension, for squabbles broke out and Jonathan found himself acting as mediator.

Jonathan did not wish to share his concerns with Ebenezer or any other officer, but his mother became his willing confidante.

"There is nothing you can do but wait, my son. David is just one man with a few followers. He can move faster than your father and his train of warriors. David will stay out of reach of the king."

"I can only hope so."

"Your father won't give up easily. Samuel's prophecy has given him cause to fear and become suspicious of any man who rises in power. David rose to the heights with one stone, and continued to add to his popularity with every victory."

"God gave him that success, Mother."

"Yes, and that adds to your father's frustration. I don't need to remind you that your future is also in the balance, Jonathan."

"My future is in God's hands, Mother. He is sovereign."

She searched his face. "You must rule in the king's absence, Jonathan. Whether Saul realizes it or not, he has left us vulnerable to our enemies."

No one knew that better than Jonathan. "Gibeah is well

protected." And he had already sent word to the outposts to keep close watch on any movement of the Philistines.

"You cannot leave things to the officers your father left behind. Who are they? What are they? You are his eldest son. The people respect you. You have fought bravely, and God has been with you. You are honest and courageous and bold."

"You make me blush with your flattery."

"I do not speak merely with the pride of a mother. You have nobility of heart, my son." She put her hand on his arm. "If anything happens to your father, you will rule, whether you wish it or not." Her eyes glowed. "And then Israel will know what it is to have a truly great king!"

"Mother, we had the greatest king in all the earth. The Lord God of Israel was our king. And He has rejected Saul. Do not put your hope in me, Mother. There will be no dynasty."

She shook her head. "Jonathan, Jonathan." Her eyes grew moist. "The Lord rejected your father. He did not reject *you*."

+ + +

A messenger arrived sweat-streaked and ashen. "I come from Nob." He trembled. "Ahimelech is dead! He is dead and every member of his family, and every priest in Nob."

Jonathan leapt to his feet. "The Philistines attacked?"

"No, my lord." He bowed his face to the ground and would not raise his head.

"The king ordered Ahimelech and his whole family killed. And then all the priests of the Lord."

"No!" Jonathan shook violently. "It can't be. *No!* Saul

couldn't. Abner wouldn't! No one would dare commit such a sin against God!"

"Abner and his men didn't, my lord. They refused to obey the king's command, but Doeg went ahead with it. He killed eighty-five men, still wearing their priestly garments! And then he put the sword to the priests' families—even the women, children, and babies in Nob. Even the infants, the cattle, the donkeys and sheep. He murdered everything in Nob that breathed!"

Jonathan cried out and tore his robe. He fell to his knees and pounded his thighs. Wrath and despair filled him. Doeg, that evildoer, disgraced God's people! Who but an Edomite would dare raise a sword against priests and their families? Who would give in to a king's mad order and carry out such evil?

His father would live to regret this. It would haunt him more than the loss of the crown and dynasty. It would plague him until he breathed his last.

In an agony of shame at what his father had commanded, Jonathan raised his arms. "May the face of the Lord turn against Doeg! May You cut off the memory of him from the earth! May his children be fatherless and his wife a widow! May his descendants be cut off, their names blotted out from the next generation!"

Even as the curses tore from his throat, Jonathan wondered how he could still love and serve the king who had ordered such an atrocity. *How can I honor this man? I am ashamed of the blood that runs in my veins!*

The Law broke his heart and burned his soul. It did not say the father had to be worthy to be honored.

"God!!"

What hope of mercy now? What hope of forgiveness for a king who murders priests? What hope for his people?

✦ ✦ ✦

King Saul returned to Gibeah under the cover of night and went out the next morning as usual to hold court.

Abner looked years older. "The people fear Saul now. They fear him more than they love David."

"It is the Lord they should fear." Jonathan turned away. He could not bear to look at his father. Not yet. He went into seclusion. He read the Law until he could not keep his eyes open and slept with the scroll in his hand.

Spies reported that David had gone to a great and defensible cave in Adullam. David's brothers and his father's entire household went down to him there. Others joined him when they heard what Saul had done to the priests of Nob and their families. Some debtors and malcontents, men of violence, and raiders joined David. Even one whole tribe, the Gadites, defected to David.

Jonathan prayed unceasingly that David would hold firm to his faith in God and do what was right in all circumstances, no matter what Saul attempted to do or what others might advise.

Keep David strong in the power of Your strength, Lord, or how will he keep those men from becoming worse than the Philistines? God, use this time to train David in faith. Give him wisdom and courage to endure! No matter what my father does, keep David faithful and within the bounds of Your perfect Law! Lord, may he never sin against You!

Saul raged. "My enemies increase with every day that passes!"

When a few Benjaminites deserted to David, Saul grew

more afraid than ever. He summoned Jonathan every
morning and kept him close. Was his own tribe about to
turn against him? "You won't desert me, will you? You're
my son, heir to my throne. You and Abner are the only
ones I can trust!"

Jonathan pitied him.

Malkishua and Abinadab, now warriors themselves,
stayed close to the king. Though they were his brothers,
Jonathan felt no true closeness with them, not as he had
with David. They saw God as their enemy and feared His
judgment. He encouraged them to study the Law, but they
"had no time for such pursuits." They were eager to bring
glory to Saul and themselves in battle, failing, as their
father had, to grasp the truth: Victory came from the Lord!

And Jonathan's mother lay dying, shame corroding her
life. She no longer desired to live and locked herself away
from everyone except Jonathan. "I'm glad he has Rizpah.
For if he called for me, I would send word I never want to
see his face again!" Jonathan saw her every day that he
was home. Then he was sent out to destroy Philistine raiders. When he returned, his mother was dead. Whether she
died by her own hand, he never heard. Nor did he ask.

Saul mourned. "Your mother wanted you to marry,
Jonathan. And so you must."

Jonathan did not want the king choosing his bride. He
would not take an idol worshiper to wife, nor anyone outside the tribe of Benjamin. She must be a virgin and a
woman of faith. He knew whom his mother had chosen,
one who met his criteria. Rachel was of the tribe of
Benjamin and a woman of excellence. She was not fasci-
nated by idols and divination, by jewels and entertain-

ments like Michal and so many others. "I will marry
Rachel, Father."

"Rachel? Who is Rachel?"

"Mother's nurse for the past two years." Clearly, the
king had not bothered to visit his queen. "She is a relative,
on Mother's side."

"Your mother comes from a long line of farmers."

"As were we, before you became king. And happier
then than now."

Saul's eyes narrowed. "We can find a much more suitable match for you than a poor farmer's daughter. After
all, you are the crown prince. One day, you will be king."

Jonathan was weary of his father's insistence that his
marriage be used to forge a military alliance. He would
marry in accordance with the Law and to please the Lord,
not his father.

"The Law is clear, Father, and I would not risk incur-
ring more of God's wrath upon our house by marrying
someone outside the tribe of Benjamin."

Saul frowned. "I suppose you are right." He smiled.
"Her father will be pleased with the match. The bride
price can be dispensed with easily enough. A year's
exemption from taxes should suffice."

"I hope you will be more generous than that, my lord."

"Two years, then. That is more than generous."

"How many years exemption did you give Rizpah's
family?" Jonathan had difficulty keeping his voice even.

Saul glared at him, his face reddened. "Do you dare to
criticize me?"

The richer his father became, the more tightly he held
the purse. While the people sacrificed to pay taxes in
order to keep Saul's army equipped and paid, the king

gave up none of his pleasures. Instead, he increased and
spread gifts and allowances among his advisors and counselors and higher officials. Did he hope to buy loyalty?
Human lusts are never satisfied!

Furious, Jonathan did not retreat from his father's glare.
"Surely King Saul can be as generous to the family of the
future princess of the realm as he was to the family of his
concubine."

His father's chin jutted. "Fine. Have your way! A royal
price for a humble bride."

Tense with anger, Jonathan bowed low. "Thank you,
my lord. May your generosity be rewarded a hundred-
fold." He could not keep the sarcasm from his voice.

"I still have three other sons who need wives. I doubt
they will be as difficult to please as you are."

"No doubt." And more laws would be broken, adding
to the sins already blackening Saul's reign.

✦   ✦   ✦

Veiled and seated on a platform, Rachel was carried to Jonathan through the throng of well-wishers. Careless of custom, he lifted her down and took her hand. It was cool and
trembled in his. "You don't need to be afraid of me," he
whispered in her ear as those around them laughed and
shouted blessings.

Wed, he lifted the veil and stared into wide, innocent
eyes, bright with tears of happiness.

When they were alone, Jonathan found himself more
afraid of her than of any man he had ever faced in battle.
He almost laughed. How was it possible that he could scale
a cliff and defeat an army of Philistines, and yet stand
trembling before this lovely, fragile girl? It took all his

courage to bend and kiss her. When she stepped easily into his embrace, her body pressed to his, he felt exalted. The sweet taste of her lifted him into the heavens.

The wedding celebration lasted a week. The people danced and sang. Jonathan wished his mother had lived to see the fulfillment of her hopes.

Ebenezer acted as Jonathan's best friend and made certain there was plenty of food and wine for everyone. But he was not David. David had been Jonathan's equal. David would have written a song for the wedding and sung it himself.

How Jonathan missed his friend! With hundreds of people celebrating his marriage, with a beautiful young wife at his side, Jonathan had never felt more lonely.

✦   ✦   ✦

God had commanded that a new husband have no work for a year so he could make his bride happy, but Jonathan and Rachel were not to have that pleasure.

David was in Keilah, fighting the Philistines who had been looting the threshing floors, and Saul saw an opportunity he could not resist.

"God has handed him over to me! David has imprisoned himself by entering a town with walls and gates!" Saul called up his forces for battle and left Jonathan to guard and administer the affairs of the kingdom in his absence.

After all this time Jonathan no longer wasted breath trying to dissuade his father from chasing David. God would protect David. Jonathan poured himself into holding the tribes together and strengthening them against the Philistines. Every morning, he rose before dawn to pray and read the Law. Only after that did he go out to administer justice to the people. He entrusted little to his father's advisors, who changed their minds with every argument. Decisions must reflect the Law he still kept tucked against his heart. Judgments must be made in reverent fear of the Lord.

A steady stream of messengers kept Jonathan apprised of what happened elsewhere. David had escaped from Keilah and was now in hiding. Jonathan gave thanksgiving offerings.

What the king had ordered in Nob haunted Jonathan.

"Keep my father from shedding more innocent blood, Lord. Guard David. Let his love and righteousness grow so that all men may see his good works and glorify You!"

Ruling for an absent king was exhausting work. Jonathan loved Rachel, but he had little time with her. His passion was for the Lord and Israel.

Standing up or sitting down, walking or practicing with his bow, or even stretched out upon his bed, Jonathan spoke to the Lord, his mind filled with hope and the possibilities if men would but turn their hearts fully to God. *Lord, You made me. You created me for such a time as this. Help me to honor my father and serve Your people. I am Your servant! Give me the sense to follow Your commands and teach the people to do likewise!*

How he longed to talk with David! He imagined the campaigns they could plan against the Philistines! If only things had turned out differently. Often, he remembered how it was to talk to David about the Lord, about battles they had fought together, about the future of Israel, twelve tribes united under one king. How many years had it been since he'd last seen his friend?

Ebenezer announced another messenger. "I don't know him, my lord. And he is a Hittite."

"I'll hear what he has to say."

Ebenezer returned with a stranger. The man bowed, but it was little more than a mockery of respect. "I am Uriah, and I have been sent with an important message for the prince." He had the rough look of a brigand, still dusty from hard travel. He hadn't bothered to wash or change his clothes before delivering his message.

"And what is your message?"

"I have brought you a gift." He took something from his pouch.

Jonathan recognized the stripes of Judah on the cloth that wrapped the gift. "Leave us!" he told his guards.

"My lord . . . ," Ebenezer protested, keeping his gaze fixed upon the sneering Hittite.

Jonathan forced a laugh. "He is but one man, and I am well armed. Do as I say."

Ebenezer left the chamber.

Jonathan crossed the room and took the small parcel. He unwrapped it and found a scroll. He read quickly, a smile blooming. A psalm of praise and hope. His eyes grew moist. "I will read it again to my wife. She will be pleased." His heart was so full, he might even sing. No, that would be a mistake. He laughed again, his heart lightened. He rolled the scroll and tucked it beneath his breastplate. "Please tell my friend that I am greatly honored and humbled by his gift."

The Hittite stood silent, studying him.

"You must eat and rest before you return. I will see that you have safe quarters. You are under my protection until you leave. Do you understand?"

Uriah bowed formally this time.

Jonathan wanted news. "How does our friend fare?"

"How would any man fare in his circumstances? He is innocent of any wrong and yet pursued by a king and an army determined to kill him."

Jonathan felt the sharp stab of guilt over his father's actions. "I pray my friend has trustworthy men around him."

"More each day, and any one of them willing to die to protect his life."

"Good."

Uriah's eyes flickered with surprise.

Jonathan met his gaze squarely. "May the Lord continue to protect him."

Uriah bowed his head. "And you, my lord prince."

"You did not answer my question."

The Hittite looked at him. "Nor will I."

"Where is he?"

"Well hidden from the hands that would take his life."

There was no reason for Uriah to trust the son of Saul, who pursued David out of jealousy. Nor would it matter to the Hittite that Jonathan had done all he could to dissuade his father from his mad pursuit. Even if he could explain, it would take too long. "I long to see him."

"He would be the better for a visit from a trusted friend."

Jonathan smiled, his mind set. "Then I will come."

"What?"

"I will go back to his camp with you."

"That would be unwise. You would be in greater danger than he is." He shook his head. "Nor can I guarantee your safety in getting there."

"Nevertheless, I will go with you." Jonathan gave the man instructions to camp in the field beside the stone pile. He gave him two shekels. "Buy what you need in the marketplace and make sure those at the gate see you leave."

After the Hittite left, Jonathan summoned Ebenezer and told him he must be "away on the king's business."

"I would go with you."

"I know you would, but you won't." Jonathan clapped a hand on Ebenezer's shoulder. "You're needed here."

"May the Lord be with you."

"And with you."

Uriah was waiting at the stone pile astride a Philistine stallion. Jonathan was impressed. "That is a fine mount you have."

Uriah grinned. He reined the horse around and came alongside Jonathan's mount. "We have taken a number of horses from the Philistines. Perhaps my master will give you one."

And how would Jonathan explain such a gift to his father, the king?

"You are alone with one of David's servants. Are you not afraid?"

Jonathan looked into the Hittite's eyes. "I travel under the protection of our mutual friend. David did not send you to assassinate me."

"He didn't tell me to bring you back either."

"That might be. But I don't believe the Lord God, who led me to rout a Philistine army at Micmash, would let me fall to one lone Hittite!" He rested one hand on the hilt of his sword. "Your manner tells me David needs encouragement."

Uriah laughed coldly. "You might say that."

"Then let's go!"

They skirted Bethlehem on the way south. Better to avoid people wherever possible so that no one would report to the king. They rode through the mountains down into the wilderness. David and his men were in Ziph.

An alarm was shouted long before they reached the camp. Men came out, armed and ready to fight, and then stood about glaring up at Jonathan as he rode into their midst. He recognized some of his kin—disgruntled, disillusioned, and defiant men who had defected from the villages of Benjamin.

"Uriah has taken Saul's son hostage!"

Men cheered, brandishing weapons. Their faces were hard, wary.

"He is no hostage!" Uriah shouted, drawing his sword. "He is David's guest. Back away!"

Joab, David's nephew and older than he by some years, stood before the rest. He flipped a Philistine knife up and down in his hand. "Greetings, Jonathan, son of King Saul." He did not address him as "my lord, the prince."

His tone set Jonathan on edge. Swinging his leg over the horse, Jonathan slid to the ground. He would not turn his back on Joab. "I come under the protection of my friend, David."

"Did he ask to speak with you?"

"*Jonathan!*"

Jonathan stepped past Joab and smiled in greeting.

Face strained, David strode toward him. "Get back! Stand away from him!" Men moved at David's command. He glowered at Joab. "The prince is my guest! See that the men are more suitably occupied."

"Yes, my lord." Joab bowed. His dark eyes glanced at Jonathan before he turned and shouted for the others to go about their business.

David turned on Uriah. "I told you to deliver a wedding gift to Prince Jonathan, not take him captive!"

"I came of my own accord, David. If Uriah had not agreed to bring me, I would have followed him." He extended his hand to Uriah. "May the Lord bless you for your kindness to me."

"And you as well, my lord." The Hittite left them alone.

David looked sick with apprehension. "You should not have come here." He glanced around pointedly. "Are you eager to die?"

"Is that any way to greet a friend?"

They embraced and slapped one another on the back. Jonathan laughed. "It has been too long, my friend." So many years had passed since last they spoke. "You have an army now."

"Your father will one day catch up with me. Sooner or later, he will hunt me down and trap me in some dank cave. He has three thousand men, the best warriors in all Israel. And I have only six hundred."

"I brought you something." Jonathan reached inside his breastplate.

"My sling!" David took it. He looked up. "But I gave it to you as a gift."

"Yes, and I'm giving it back to you. Do you remember the last time you used that?"

"The day I killed Goliath."

"You were not afraid that day, and your courage rallied every Israelite who witnessed what you did. The Lord gave us victory."

"I was a boy, then, racing into battle with the belief that the Lord was with me."

"And so He was."

"The Lord has forsaken me."

Jonathan understood now why he had felt impelled to see David. "Ah, my friend, the Lord has not abandoned you. And it is better to be a poor but wise youth than an old and foolish king who refuses all advice." He smiled sadly. "Such a youth could come from the sheep pastures and succeed. He might even become king, though he was born to poverty. Everyone is eager to help such a youth, even to help him take the throne."

David stared at him. "Surely you know better. I don't want the throne!"

"Neither did my father. Once. Long ago. Now, he hangs on to it with every fiber of his strength and wields fear like a whip over God's people."

"Why are you saying these things to me?"

Jonathan wanted to say more, but he didn't want to speak before David's men and plant thoughts of rebellion. It was one thing to run *from* a king, another to run *after* him. "Can we leave your camp and walk a while? Alone?"

David gave orders to his guards. They didn't look pleased as they walked way, but they kept their distance.

"What am I to do, Jonathan? You know I've never done anything against the king." Tears flowed. "I have served him with everything I had. And yet he hates me! He hunts me like an animal! Everywhere I go, someone betrays me and sends word to Saul. They seek a reward for my life. And I must live with men who live by violence, men I barely trust."

Jonathan was reminded of his father as he listened to

David's outburst. Tempestuous. Filled with fear. *Steady him, Lord.* "Don't be afraid, David. Trust in the Lord and the power of His strength to protect you. My father will never find you!"

"How can you be so sure?"

It was time to speak what he knew in his heart. "Did Samuel not anoint you king years ago in Bethlehem?"

Color surged into David's cheeks. "How did you know?"

"It was obvious that you were God's servant the first time I heard you sing in my father's house. And when you went down to face Goliath, and all the times you fought against the enemies of the Lord. When we sat and studied the Law together, I knew you were a man after God's own heart. You *are* going to be the king of Israel, and I will be next to you, as my father, Saul, is well aware. The Lord is our rock. He is your deliverer." He gave a soft laugh. "What a pity I cannot play the harp and sing songs that will fill you with hope."

Jonathan spread his hands. "I have spent hours— days—thinking about what you're going through, consumed with guilt because it is my father who causes you trouble. And I must believe that the battles you're facing now aren't coming to you apart from God."

"Then where is He?"

"The Lord watches over you, David. He sees your coming out and going in. He is training you for a higher purpose. My father, even now, is being given opportunities to repent, and it grieves me beyond words to watch his heart grow harder with every test he faces." His voice broke.

David put his hand upon his arm.

Jonathan swallowed hard. "May your heart soften like

rich, plowed earth in which God will plant His seeds of truth and wisdom." He spoke with conviction. "God has not forsaken you, David, nor will He. Not as long as you hold fast to Him and you walk—or run—in His ways."

David relaxed. His muscles loosened, and he smiled faintly. "I have missed you, Jonathan. I have missed your counsel."

Jonathan's throat closed.

David looked out over his camp. "You see the sort of men I command. Fugitives. Malcontents. Men bent on violence. I hate living like this!"

"If you could rule such men and turn their hearts toward God, what a king you would be!"

David kept his face turned away. "They urge me to fight back, to kill your father and destroy the house of Saul."

It was the custom of the nations around them.

Jonathan spoke carefully. "God anointed my father king, but He anointed you as well. What does the Law say?"

David grew pensive. He closed his eyes. "'You must not murder.'"

"So what does that leave you?"

"I must wait."

"And teach your men to wait upon the Lord as well." He went to David and stood with him, looking out over the wilderness. "No one can truly lead men until he learns to follow God."

David smiled ruefully. "I never thought it would be this difficult."

Jonathan put his hand on David's shoulder and squeezed. "Do what you know is right, what we talked about all those evenings we read the Law together so many years ago. Do not repay evil for evil. Don't retaliate when my father and those who follow him tell lies about you. Do good for the people. That is what God wants you to do, no matter what your circumstances."

"You see the way I live. From hand to mouth. Running, always running."

Jonathan wept. "I can only tell you what I know. The eyes of the Lord watch over those who do right, and His ears are open to your prayers. The Lord turns His face from evil. I have watched how God has turned from my father because Saul rejected Him. The Law tells me to honor my father. It does not say honor him only if he is honorable." His sorrow sometimes pulled him down into despair.

"I walk a narrow path, David, between a king whose heart grows harder with every year that passes and a friend who will be king. But I will keep to it in obedience to the Lord. A man who lives by his own light and warms himself by his own fire one day will lie down in eternal torment. Such is the life my father leads, David, seeing enemies where there are none, hungry and thirsty for the Word of God and not even knowing it. His every act of disobedience widens the gap between himself and the One who can give him peace: the Lord!"

Jonathan raised his hands in anguish. "Lord, I do not want to follow my father. I long to follow after You, to be where You are. Don't You jealously long for Your people to be faithful? Surely You offer us the strength we need to keep faith. Give us strength!"

David looked at him, eyes awash. "I had not thought how this must be for you."

Jonathan's shoulders relaxed. His mouth tipped. "You've had other things on your mind. Surviving, for one."

"But what about you, Jonathan? You are the prince of Israel, heir to your father's throne."

"Don't make the same mistake my father has. It's not my father's throne. It's God's throne to give to whomever He chooses. And the Lord sent Samuel to anoint *you* the next king of Israel." He wanted David to understand. "I love my father, David, but I'm not proud of him. When I heard what he ordered at Nob, I was ashamed of the blood that runs in my veins."

David spoke in a quick rush of words. "It was my fault that happened, Jonathan. I saw Doeg. If I'd killed that Edomite, none of those priests would have died. Their wives and children would still live." He nodded toward the camp. "Ahimelech's son, Abiathar, is with us and under our protection."

"My father gave the order. What Saul does in the name of his kingship makes my bones ache with shame." He lowered his head and fought his emotions. "I pray unceasingly that my father will repent. We would both know if that happened. He would remove the crown from his head and place it on yours."

How different Israel would be if his father returned to the Lord.

If only, Lord. If only . . .

"You came a long way to see me, my friend." David spoke quietly, his voice hoarse with emotion. "Come. Eat. Rest."

"I came to encourage you."

"We will encourage one another." David slapped him

on the back as they headed back to camp. "We will sing songs of deliverance to our God. We will praise the Lord together." He grinned. "We will make joyful noise before the Lord."

Jonathan laughed. Here was the David he remembered and loved so dearly, the friend who was closer than a brother.

They did celebrate far into the night.

And David's men watched in wonder.

+   +   +

When Jonathan awakened, he saw David stretched out across the entrance to the tent. He sat up and David awakened, reaching for the sword at his side. "We're safe, David. All is well." And then it occurred to Jonathan what David had been doing. "Am I a lamb that you must sleep at the gate of the sheepfold?"

"My men—"

"You don't have to explain." He gave David a nod and grinned. "I am honored to have the commander of such an army as my personal bodyguard."

David called for his servant to bring food. They breakfasted together.

"You eat well."

David shrugged. "Some of the people are good to us."

"Be careful whom you trust. Even though you delivered Keilah from raiders, they were only too eager to turn you over to Saul."

David nodded, pensive. "How is Michal?"

Jonathan felt the heat mount in his cheeks. Michal was like those of Keilah. Fickle and shallow, she had nothing good to say about David. Jonathan shook his head. "She is well and lives alone." He didn't want to speak against his sister.

David looked grim. "This is no place for a woman like Michal. We're always on the run."

"One day you will come home, David."

"For now, I must live in the wilderness."

"Remember our history. The wilderness is a sacred place to our people. God called us into the wilderness. It was in the wilderness God met with our forefathers and traveled with them. It was in the wilderness God performed His great miracles."

"It is a barren, difficult place where every day is a challenge to the body and soul."

"The wilderness refined the faith of our forefathers and prepared them to enter the Promised Land. It is in the wilderness that you will learn God is sovereign. The Lord will meet your needs. He will train you as He trained Joshua and Caleb. God prepared them for battle and gave them victory. Surely, God's voice is heard more easily here in the quiet than in the cacophony of a king's court."

David grinned. "And yet you would make a king of me."

"Only great men like Moses have the wisdom to follow on the heels of God." Jonathan rose. "It is time for me to return to Gibeah."

David helped him with his breastplate.

Jonathan strapped on his sword. Grief welled up in him as he looked at David's face. "The king has left me in command of the kingdom while he—" He could not speak. How many years might pass before he saw his friend again?

"Stay with me, Jonathan!"

"I can't. But I will never raise my hand against you. I will do all I can to guard the kingdom and teach the people to revere the prophets and obey the Law." He embraced David. "I must go."

They went out together and Jonathan faced David's men. He saw death in their faces, an eagerness to conquer. Jonathan turned to David and they clasped hands. "If anything happens to me, David, protect my wife and children."

"You have a child?"

"Not yet, but God willing, I hope to have as many as the arrows in my quiver."

"May the Lord so bless you. You have my word, Jonathan. I will protect your wife and children."

Jonathan bowed at the waist as he would to the king.

Uriah stood holding the reins of the horse. Jonathan took them and mounted. "I know the way back."

"May the Lord your God watch over and protect you."

Jonathan looked at David, raised his hand in fellowship, and then rode away alone.

+   +   +

King Saul returned to Gibeah, morbid and glum. Jonathan relinquished his duties beneath the tamarisk tree and turned his attention to strengthening the tribes.

Months passed.

Ziphites came. David was hiding among them in the strongholds of Horesh. They would hand David over to Saul if the king came down to capture him.

"I have also received reports, Father. David has protected their flocks and herds. What reason have they to betray David? Do not trust these men. They are too eager

to take you away from Gibeah." His arguments merely
delayed Saul's departure and planted more seeds of suspicion.

"The Lord bless you," Saul told the Ziphite messengers.
"At last someone is concerned about me! Go and check
again to be sure of where he is staying and who has seen
him there, for I know that he is very crafty. Discover his
hiding places, and come back when you are sure. Then I'll
go with you. And if he is in the area at all, I'll track him
down, even if I have to search every hiding place in
Judah!"

Jonathan sent Ebenezer to warn David against the
Ziphites.

But before the week was over, Saul summoned his warriors and headed south into Judah's territory.

✦   ✦   ✦

Jonathan awakened in the middle of the night. His body
streamed sweat, his heart pounded. He had dreamed that
his father was riding along one side of a mountain with his
warriors while David and his men were on the other side
running for their lives. The king had them trapped and
outnumbered.

Someone pounded on his door.

Rachel awakened beside him. "What is it?"

Jonathan threw his clothes on. "I'll send your maid. Bar
the door until I return." He ran out the door, shouting to
the servants.

Ebenezer had come for him. "The Philistines are heading this way, my lord."

"Send word to King Saul! Tell him, 'Come quickly! The

Philistines are attacking!'" Jonathan strapped on his sword as he ran.

Perhaps it was a blessing in disguise.

The wandering king would have to come home. For now. But Jonathan knew that as soon as the immediate crisis subsided, his father would once again resume his mad quest to kill David.

AS Jonathan had feared, King Saul continued after David even as the Philistine threat grew. "He's gone to En-gedi. I have him now! I'll get him this time!"

Year after year, the chase went on, Saul never tiring of the hunt.

"Let him go, Father! We must keep our eyes upon the Philistines! Would you have them overrun the land and put the yoke of slavery around our necks? Israel needs you here!"

"What good if I am no longer king?"

Saul took his contingent of three thousand and went after David once again, hunting him and the growing numbers following him near the rocks of the wild goats.

Left to defend the kingdom, Jonathan sent for representatives from the tribes to gather and discuss defense tactics. He worked night and day, hearing reports, sending out warriors to strengthen defenses, and soothing the people's fears.

When Saul again returned home, unsuccessful, he compounded his sins by arranging a marriage between Michal and Palti, the son of Laish.

"You cannot do this, Father! You'll make her an adulteress!"

"Palti is besotted with your sister. I can use that to my advantage. If Michal were not agreeable to the match, I might hesitate."

Jonathan knew he argued in vain, and sent a message to Samuel, pleading that the seer come and speak to the king. When Samuel did not answer, Jonathan went to his sister, but she was far from mourning the arrangement. As far as she was concerned, David had deserted her.

"Why shouldn't I have some happiness? David is such a coward! All he does is run and hide in caves like a wild animal."

"Would you prefer he defended himself and killed our father?"

"Why should I spend the rest of my life without a husband, locked away in my chambers?"

"You *have* a husband! David is your husband!"

"Then where is he? Does he send me love songs? Does he long for me as I longed for him for years? He doesn't care about me. He never did. He thought our marriage would put him a step closer to the throne." She lifted her chin. "Besides, Father wants me to marry Palti and I'm going to obey. And Palti is far more handsome than David."

"Is that all you care about, Michal? What the man looks like?"

Her eyes darkened. "Palti loves me! Have you seen how he looks at me? We will have many fine sons. Beautiful, strong sons. I will help build up Saul's house!"

"Be careful how you talk, little sister. One day, David *will* be king."

"You speak treason against the king, our father!"

"Father knows. Samuel told him that God had chosen another. It's why Saul hates David so much, why he pursues him relentlessly. But God will prevail—"

"God! God! All you ever think about is God."

"David will reign, Michal. If you wait, you will be his queen. If you go through with this marriage, what do you suppose David will do with you when he returns?"

The fire went out of her eyes. She turned away and lifted her shoulders. "David will take me back." She faced him again. "I will tell him King Saul *commanded* me to marry, and I had no choice in the matter. It's true, after all."

"It won't matter. According to the Law, you will be defiled. David will never sleep with you again."

"He will!"

"No, he won't."

She burst into tempestuous tears. "It's not my fault what plans are made for me."

She sickened him. "You go into this marriage as a willing participant!"

"You care more about that wretched shepherd than you do about your own sister!"

"You, my sister, are no better than a harlot who gives herself to the highest bidder and prostitutes herself before idols!"

Stunned, she stared at him, fear filling her eyes. "I loved David. You know I loved him." Angry color surged into her cheeks. "And what good did it do me? Do I have sons? It's so easy for you to condemn me. You have a wife. Soon you will have a son!"

Her mouth twisted as she spat bitter venom. "She'll probably have a dozen sons and daughters for you, perfect as you are. God's delight! Firstborn son and the delight of the king! And what hope have I ever to have a son of my own? Tell me that, brother. If David won't defend himself against father, then he's destined to run and keep running for however many years father lives. And Father is a strong man, isn't he? I'll be an old woman by the time David returns, if he returns. Too old to have children!

I hate him! I hate the life I live because of him! *I wish Father would kill him and we'd all be done with it!"*

"May the Lord reveal the truth about you!" Jonathan left, vowing never to look upon his sister's face again.

+   +   +

Saul returned once again and retreated into his house. Only Jonathan and the king's most trusted personal servants were allowed close. Saul paid little attention to matters of state. He sat brooding, chin in hand, face sallow, dejected as Jonathan went over the reports that came in from the tribes. Only maps of the regions interested him, especially those showing areas in which David lived.

Frustrated, Jonathan summoned Abner. "What happened at the rocks of the wild goats to put the king in such a foul mood?"

A muscle twitched in the commander's jaw. "We almost captured David. We were so close. We just didn't realize how close."

"What do you mean?"

Abner looked embarrassed. "The king needed to relieve himself. He went into a cave while guards stood outside, keeping watch. When the king returned, we were ready to set off again and then David appeared."

"Where?"

"At the entrance to the cave. He and his men had been inside with the king." His eyes darkened. "How they must have laughed."

"What did David do?"

"He called down to us. He said his men had encouraged him to kill Saul."

"Joab and his brothers, no doubt." Jonathan could

imagine those men urging David to take advantage of the moment, murder the king and take the crown for himself.

"What did David say?"

Abner's jaw clenched. "He said a lot of things." The commander glowered, lips pressed tight.

"Tell me everything, Abner."

"He said he'd spared the king because Saul is God's anointed. But he had cut away a piece of your father's robe to prove how close he had been. Of course, he claimed he was innocent of any wrong. And then he cried out for the Lord to judge between him and your father, and prayed that God would take revenge for all the wrongs he claims the king has done to him." Abner sneered. "Oh, of course, David swore his hand would not touch the king. He said, 'From evil people come evil deeds.' He dared speak as though your father were the interloper. That man has done more damage to your father than any Philistine ever hoped to do!"

"And what damage would that be, Abner, when Saul broke faith with David?"

"Your loyalty must be with your father."

"It is! Am I not here running the kingdom while he runs after David? Have I not proven my loyalty year after year?"

"David humiliated Saul before his men. Do you not call that damage? You could have spared your father long ago. You had opportunity after opportunity to destroy his enemy."

"David is not the king's enemy!"

Abner leaned close, furious. "Saul wept aloud! And then he confessed loud enough for all of us to hear! He said that miserable Judean shepherd is a better man than he. Saul said he had treated David badly and David had returned nothing but good."

Tears sprang to Jonathan's eyes, tears of joy, but Abner didn't understand. He and David's relative Joab had much in common. "The Lord delivered King Saul into David's hands, and David honored him."

"Honor?" Abner's eyes darkened. "What honor did he show when he cut into the royal vestments? Where is the honor when men hide in the darkness to snigger at the king who seeks privacy for his most personal needs?!"

"Where is the honor in hunting down a man who has done nothing but serve king and people?" Abner drew back at Jonathan's words, eyes fierce. Jonathan held his stare. "No answer to that, Abner? Then how about this? Did you send warriors into the cave *before* my father went in?"

Abner flushed deep red.

"Perhaps it is your own failure to do your duty that angers you most. You failed to protect the king."

Abner's eyes grew colder. "It might interest you to hear that King Saul said the Lord would reward *David* for his treatment. King Saul said *David* would surely be king and that the kingdom of Israel would flourish under *his* rule. You were not mentioned, my prince. Although King Saul did beg David not to murder all his descendants and wipe his family from the face of the earth."

Jonathan smiled. "David follows the Law of the Lord our God. He does not follow the customs of the nations around us."

"Then why are they now his allies?"

+ + +

Samuel died. King Saul and all Israel assembled to mourn
for him. King Saul spoke to the throng of people. The king
spoke glowing words of praise for the seer, and led the
procession to the prophet's resting place.

Jonathan had insisted that raisin cakes be given to the
people before they returned home. Some had come great
distances to pay Samuel respect. Saul had groaned loudly,
claiming such gifts would impoverish him, but Jonathan
persisted. "A generous king is loved by his people. The
people will pay their taxes more willingly when they
know the king has an open hand in their regard."

The king sat on a dais beneath an elaborate canopy and
watched the crowds. He was looking for one man: David.
He had stationed men throughout in case David appeared.
Abner made certain if David did come, there would be no
escape.

Thousands filed past the stacks of cakes, receiving their
allotment. Jonathan spoke blessings and words of encouragement to those who came through his line.

A man dressed in rags and bent with years hobbled
forward. His head covered, his beard dusty, he leaned
heavily on a crooked cane. His head bobbed in repeated
bows as he mumbled.

Jonathan stepped closer and supported the man's arm
as he gave him a raisin cake.

"My lord the prince is most kind to his people," the
man murmured.

"It is the kindness of God who gives us the wheat and
the grapes to make these cakes. Praise His name."

The man took the proffered raisin cake, shoved it into

his pouch, and grasped Jonathan's hand. His grip was not that of an old man. "May the Lord bless you for your generosity, my son." David lifted his head just enough that their gazes met.

Jonathan held firmly to David's hand. "And may the Lord God of Abraham, Isaac, and Jacob protect you in your travels."

✦   ✦   ✦

The Philistines raided the land once again, and Saul and Jonathan led warriors to fight.

When the Ziphites reported that David was hiding on the hill of Hakilah that faced Jeshimon, Saul turned aside, took Abner and his three thousand chosen warriors of Benjamin, and went after him, leaving Jonathan to drive the Philistines back. Ebenezer, now one of Jonathan's most trusted commanders, remained to protect Gibeah.

When Jonathan returned home, he learned that Rachel had given birth to their first child. But infection had set in, and Rachel was dying. "Nothing can be done, my lord," he was told.

Jonathan went to her.

"Your son." Rachel gazed at the baby in the crook of her arm. "So beautiful. Like his father." Her breath was faint. She looked at the nurse standing close by, who, weeping, leaned down and took the infant.

Jonathan's throat closed. He was filled with regrets. He loved his wife, but Israel had always been his passion. Not once had Rachel complained. Now, she wore the pallor of approaching death. He struggled with guilt. "He is perfect, Rachel. A gift from the Lord." His voice caught in his

throat. He took his wife's hand and kissed the palm.
"Thank you."

"Jonathan. Do not look so sad, my love." She could
barely whisper. "The people need you." He leaned down
so that her lips were against his ear. "Our son must have
a proper name."

His eyes filled. "Try to rest."

"No time," she whispered. "Merib-baal is a good
name."

One who contends against idols. Jonathan couldn't speak.
He held her hand tighter.

Her fingers moved weakly. "Or Mephibosheth."

*One who would destroy the shame of idol worship in
Israel.* Jonathan could only nod. *Let it be so, Lord. May my
son rise up to praise Your Name.* He kissed Rachel's hand
again and held it cradled tenderly between his own. She
sighed softly, the light fading from her eyes. He closed
them with shaking fingers and wept.

He did not leave her chambers until morning light. He
washed, prayed, gave offerings as the Law prescribed, and
then returned to the increasingly difficult duties of a
prince guarding the realm for an absent king.

✦ ✦ ✦

Jonathan kept his son close as he grew. He read the Law
aloud to Merib-baal even as a babe still in the arms of a
nurse. When Jonathan held court beneath the tamarisk
tree, he held Merib-baal in his lap as he heard cases and
made judgments in accordance with God's law. When the
child grew restless, Jonathan gave the boy over to his
nurse.

When Merib-baal began to walk, he toddled among the

elders and counselors. Jonathan wanted Merib-baal accustomed to the counsel of men. His son must have no fear when voices were raised in disagreement. For one day, God willing, his son would have a place among the council and would fight for the abolition of all idols from Israel.

Jonathan made a miniature bow and arrows for his son and patiently taught him how to shoot into a basket.

Merib-baal wanted to go everywhere Jonathan did, and was often seen out in the field, watching and playing as his father practiced with his bow.

"You cannot go with me to war, my son." Perhaps, one day, when his son was grown, he would have to go, but Jonathan prayed continually that Israel would conquer their enemies and end the wars. He prayed that his son's generation could sit without fear beneath their olive trees and watch their crops grow. But the day when King Saul rested peacefully with his forefathers—and Jonathan stood beside the next king, David—was a dream yet to come.

Jonathan continued his work to unite the tribes against their common enemy, the Philistines. He urged his younger brothers to follow God rather than men. He pressed his father to repent and trust in the God who had called him to be king over Israel.

And often he despaired, for his efforts changed little. Least of all the heart of a jealous king, or of the king's youngest sons.

✦   ✦   ✦

Yet again, Saul heard reports of David's hiding place, and prepared to go after his sworn enemy.

"David spares your life time and again!" Jonathan reminded him, knowing it was futile.

"Only to humiliate me!"

"He has sworn he will not raise a hand against you."

"Should I believe such a vow when he gathers an army around him? He will never raise his hand against me because I will kill him first!"

"How many years will it take before you realize David will never fight against you?"

Deaf to all reason, Saul stormed out.

Abner looked grim. Was he growing weary of this chase? "If anything happens to your father, I will make sure the crown is placed upon your head and no other."

"The crown will go to the man God chooses."

"And why wouldn't God choose you? The people love you. You look like a king. You tend the people like a king. It would be to everyone's advantage if you *were* king."

Jonathan went cold. *God, spare us from ambitious men!* He gripped the neck of Abner's breastplate and yanked the commander forward. Nose to nose, he spoke in a low voice. "If my father falls, Abner, you had better fall with him!"

+   +   +

The outposts Jonathan had established sent out warriors to keep watch over the Philistines. Jonathan pored over maps, afraid of what the future held.

Reports came more frequently. "King Saul returns from the wilderness of Ziph."

Relieved, Jonathan went out to greet his father at the gate. Saul came toward Gibeah, head down, shoulders slumped, riding well in front of his officers.

"May the Lord bless your homecoming, my lord." Jonathan bowed low. As he raised his head, he saw a look on his father's face that gave him hope that the long years of chasing David were at an end.

Saul dismounted and embraced him. "I trust no one but you, my son!" He cast a quick glance at Abner and turned to the elders who had come to welcome him home.

Jonathan followed the king to his palace.

As soon as he was out of sight of the welcoming crowds, King Saul kicked over urns and shouted at the servants to get out of his sight. Even Rizpah, the king's mistress, fled. Saul flung himself onto his throne and buried his head in his hands. "I can trust no one." He groaned as though in terrible pain.

"What happened in the wilderness, Father?"

Moaning, he gripped his head. "David! *I hate the very name!*" He surged to his feet. "I awoke one night with him shouting down at me. I thought I was dreaming, but there he was, standing on the hill across from our camp. David said Abner deserved to die for not protecting me. Abner and all his men deserved to die." Saul paced.

Jonathan offered him a goblet of wine to calm him, but the king threw it across the room.

"'Look around!' David said. 'Where are the king's spear and the jug of water that were beside his head?' He held up my water jug and spear!" Saul trembled as he looked at Jonathan. "Tell me! How is it possible for a man to walk through three thousand men and reach me? Is he a sorcerer? Is he a ghost? Or do my own warriors hope he will kill me?"

"Father—"

Exasperated, Saul raised his hands in the air. "I cried

out to him, 'Is that you, my son David?'" His eyes grew wild. "I called him *my son*. And he demanded to know why I'm pursuing him. He demanded to know what he had done, what crime he was guilty of. He accused my servants of inciting me against him! And he cursed them! He claims they've driven him from his home and the inheritance God promised him. He said they hoped he would serve other gods. He cried out that I must not allow him to die on foreign soil, far from the presence of the Lord."

Saul's face twisted in an agony of frustration as he continued. "He said I had come out to look for a flea as I would hunt a partridge in the mountains!" He sank onto his throne and sobbed. "If he were a flea, I would have crushed him long ago!"

Jonathan pitied his father. Pride goeth before a fall.

Saul pounded his knees. "I said I would not harm him. I said I had been a fool and very, very wrong." His eyes were black holes of despair. "And he would not come to me! *He would not come!* He threw *my* spear so that it was between us and ordered one of *my* men to get it. Do you see how he taunts me? And then he said the Lord gives His own reward for doing good and for being loyal. He boasted that the Lord had placed me in his power and he had refused to kill me."

Saul held his head, eyes shut, as though he wanted to crush the words echoing in his mind. "David said, 'Now may the Lord value my life, even as I have valued yours today. May He rescue me from all my troubles.'"

"David will never raise his hand against you, Father."

Saul rose. "He won't have to when the kingdom goes after him. All my men watched. I could do nothing but bless my enemy." His mouth twisted as he spat out bitter words. "'You will do many heroic deeds, and you will surely succeed.' I said that to him and then he turned his back on me and went away. *He turned his back on me!*" He pounded his chest. "I am king! No matter what Samuel said, I hold the power! I—" The madness suddenly went out of his eyes and he looked frightened. "How did David come so close? He must have stood over me, my own spear in his hand."

"And yet, did not kill you."

Saul didn't seem to hear. "Abner was right beside me. My men were all around me. Sleeping! Or were they? Maybe they watched and hoped David would kill me."

"It is the Lord who allowed David to come close to you. The Lord has given you another opportunity to repent."

Saul's head came up. "Repent?" Saul shook his head. "I've done nothing wrong. God chose me to be king! Is it not right that a king should protect his kingdom?" He clenched his hands. "Why won't you go out with me against my enemy David? He would come to you, Jonathan, and I could kill him. And then this rebellion would all be over! You're my son, heir to my throne! Why won't you fight to hold on to what belongs to us?"

Long ago, Samuel had told Jonathan to speak the truth, even when the king wouldn't want to hear it. "I will fight beside you against any enemy of Israel. But David is not one of them."

"David is my worst enemy!" Saul's face contorted in rage. "David must die!"

Years of frustration and crushed hope ripped away the walls of restraint. Furious, Jonathan cried out. "Lies and deceit! All of it! *You are your own worst enemy! Pride rules your heart and we all suffer for it!*"

Eyes wide, Saul sank back into his throne. "Is it not enough that God hates me? Now my own son—my favorite, my heir—hates me, too?" When not shouting like a madman, Saul whined like a child.

"I don't hate you. God knows! I honor you. You're my father. But I have watched the Lord give you chance after chance, and you continue to reject Him!"

Saul put his fists over his eyes. "The Lord has clothed me in disgrace!" His mouth trembled.

An inexplicable compassion filled Jonathan. Words of the Law filled his mind and heart: *The Lord is slow to anger and rich in unfailing love, forgiving every kind of sin and rebellion.* "The Lord forgives those who turn back to Him." The promise of a dynasty was gone, but surely peace with God was worth more than any crown upon a man's head! "Return to the Lord, Father, for if you don't, the Lord will not allow your sin to go unpunished. The Lord will punish the children for the sins of their parents to the third and fourth generation. Your rebellion against God will cause Merib-baal and all his cousins to suffer!"

"I'm tired." Saul let out a heavy breath. "I'm so tired of chasing after David . . ."

"Then *stop!*"

Saul looked up at him, his eyes glistening. "You will make a fine king one day. Far better than I."

"I do not wish to rule, Father—only to serve." Jonathan went down on one knee before his father. "When a man loves the Lord God of Israel with all his heart, mind, soul, and strength, perhaps then he may ask for the desire of his heart."

Saul's expression softened. "What do you desire, my son?"

"I want to destroy the Philistines. I want to drive God's enemies from our land. I want to unite our people beneath one king, the king God has anointed. I want our people to be at peace with God!"

"You want God back on the throne."

"Yes!" With all his heart, Jonathan wished it could be so.

✦   ✦   ✦

David escaped to Philistia with his army and lived in Gath under the protection of King Achish. David had two wives with him. One had brought him an alliance with Jezreel, and the other, the great wealth of Nabal of Carmel.

Jonathan grieved at the reports he heard. Had David forgotten the Law? The Law said a king was not to have multiple wives! Women would divide his heart. Had the years of fleeing Saul made David value military alliances over obeying the Lord their God?

"So much for your friend's loyalty. He beds down with our enemies," Saul said.

"And may return with information we sorely need."

Saul shook his head, refusing to believe any good of David. "If he learns the secret to forging iron, he will use it to make weapons against us."

Abner looked at Jonathan grimly. "Achish has given David Ziklag."

Saul raged. "He is out of my reach living in Philistine territory."

Anger welled in Jonathan. "It will please you both to remember that Goliath was from Gath. David will be no more welcome in Gath than he is in Judah."

"I had forgotten." Saul laughed. "Goliath's relatives will serve me well if they kill him."

Jonathan knew better. Not even Goliath's relatives would last long against David and his mighty men. The Lord protected them.

✦   ✦   ✦

Over the ensuing months, Jonathan heard rumors. David went out on raids and returned with sheep and cattle, donkeys and camels. But none of the villages that had been raided in Israel had seen David.

Jonathan remembered how he and David had plotted raids upon the Geshurites, Girzites, and Amalekites, enemies of Israel from ancient times. The Amalekites had been the worst of all, murdering the weak and weary stragglers who could not keep up with the slaves fleeing Egypt.

Jonathan suspected where David gained his wealth. But the raids added to the danger David was in. Being familiar with the Hebrew songs honoring David for killing his tens of thousands, the Philistine commanders would have no reason to trust David! And knowing that David ran from Saul, they'd wonder what better way to prove himself and win back Saul's favor than by betraying his hosts, the Philistines.

Jonathan laughed at David's boldness, as David grew rich from raiding Philistine villages while living under the protection of the king! Surely the Lord laughed as well. David would have time now to learn the secrets of forging iron.

Not a doubt regarding his friend entered Jonathan's mind. One day, David would return to Israel, and he would bring with him the resources and knowledge gained from the Philistines.

The only question was whether the Lord would allow David to return in time to save Saul from his own miscalculations.

✦   ✦   ✦

Heading for Aphek, the Philistines gathered their forces, and Jonathan feared they brought God's judgment with them.

Jonathan lifted Merib-baal onto his shoulders and went out into the fields. "Run, Abba! Run!" Merib-baal spread his arms like an eagle and squealed with laughter as Jonathan ran.

Reaching the stone pile, Jonathan lifted his son down and set him upon his feet. "I must go away again, my son."

"Me go, too.'

"No."

"Don't go." Merib-baal wrapped his arms around Jonathan's neck and clung.

Jonathan held him tight and then pried his son's arms loose and held them at his side. "Stand still. You must listen now, Merib-baal. This is important. Look at me!" The boy raised his tear-streaked face. "Remember what I've taught you. Always worship the Lord our God with all your heart, mind, soul, and strength."

Jonathan touched his son's chest and forehead, and ran his hands down his son's arms. He struggled against the emotions filling him. Was his son too young yet to understand? *Lord, make him understand. Open his heart to my words.*

Digging his fingers into the earth, Jonathan took Merib-baal's hand. He poured soil into it. "This is land the Lord our God gave to us. It is our inheritance. We are God's people. Your abba must go away and fight to make sure no one takes it from us. Do you understand?"

"I don't want you to go." Merib-baal had his mother's eyes. Doe eyes filled with innocence and sorrow.

Oh, God, protect my son! The boy's weeping pierced Jonathan's heart. Jonathan knew there was always a chance he might not return. He had never talked of David with his son before, but perhaps he was old enough now. He had to be old enough. He held Merib-baal away. "Do you know who David is?"

"Enemy."

"No. No, Merib-baal. You must listen to me. David is my friend. He is your friend, too." Jonathan cupped his son's face. "Remember this, Merib-baal. One day you will meet David. When you do, I want you to bow down to him. Bow down with your face to the ground the way men do before Grandfather. God has chosen David to be the next king over Israel. David will be your king. Do whatever David asks of you. Be his friend as your abba has been his friend. Don't make him sad."

Merib-baal nodded.

Lifting his son, Jonathan swung him back onto his shoulders and headed back to Gibeah.

The child's nurse waited at the city gate and followed them to the house.

Jonathan put his son down, hugged and kissed him. He buried his face in the side of his son's neck, inhaling his scent.

Merib-baal's arms tightened around his neck. "I love you, Abba."

Jonathan's heart lurched. "I love you, too, my son." He combed his fingers through the thick curly locks of soft hair. "Practice with your bow. Listen to the reading of God's law every day." Jonathan had made arrangements for it to be read in his absence. "Go now and play while I speak with your nurse." He straightened, watching his son scamper off.

"If you should hear that the Philistines have defeated us, hide my son quickly. Do you understand?" The Philistines would sweep across the land, hunting down all of Saul's relatives and putting them to the sword if they could.

"Yes, my lord."

He saw the nurse understood. "Do as I've instructed. Do not wait for the counsel of others. Get Merib-baal away from Gibeah. Keep him safe until David becomes king. Then take my son to him."

"But, my lord—"

"You need not fear David." Jonathan prepared to leave. "He and I made a covenant of friendship. David will keep his oath."

+   +   +

Jonathan saw terror in his father's eyes when the king heard that a great multitude of Philistine warriors was headed for Shunem, and David was sighted among their numbers, marching at the rear with King Achish.

Saul turned to Jonathan. "Your friend fights for our enemies now."

"Never." Jonathan remained convinced. "When the

battle begins, King Achish will be the first to fall, and
David will attack the Philistines from the rear."

Abner looked grim. "If that happens, we may have
a chance."

Without David's help, there was no hope. The
Philistines vastly outnumbered the Israelites. Deserters
had bled Saul's army, and swollen the ranks of David's.
Even the tribe of Manasseh and some from Benjamin had
joined David. He led a great army now, like the army of
God.

"We will camp at Gilboa."

✦ ✦ ✦

When Jonathan stood on the hill above the Philistines'
camp at Shunem, he drew his breath. His heart sank.
There were so many warriors, as many as the grains of
sand on the seashore.

Beside him, Saul stared, appalled. "We are undone."
He backed away. "I must . . . pray. I must inquire of the
Lord." When Jonathan turned to follow, Saul shook his
head. "Go and see to our men, Jonathan. Encourage them.
Abner will assist you."

It was nightfall before Jonathan returned from his mission, and his father was nowhere to be found. Jonathan
went to the king's priests. "Where is Saul?"

"He left with two of his attendants."

It was close to dawn when the king returned to his tent,
disguised as a commoner. Jonathan thought he was an
intruder and drew his sword, but the king threw off his
disguise and sank to his bed, his attendants melting away
into the darkness.

"What does all this mean?" Jonathan grew alarmed. "Where have you been?"

Saul buried his head in his hands. "Endor."

"Endor! Why would you go there?"

"To learn what will happen in the battle."

Jonathan felt a wave of fear sweep over him. "What have you done?"

Saul lifted his head, wild-eyed. "Inquired of a sorceress."

"No." Jonathan shut his eyes. *"No!"*

"I had to speak to Samuel. I had to raise him from the dead. And only she had the power to do it!"

"You know it is forbidden!" Jonathan covered his head in shame. "As God required! You expelled the mediums and spiritualists from Israel."

"She conjured the prophet from his grave!" Saul cried out.

"And did you get your answer? You have killed us all!" Jonathan wanted to grab his father and shake him. "Even now you rebel against the Lord. You bring God's wrath upon us!"

"I had to know what would happen tomorrow. Samuel was angry. He wanted to know why I bothered him now that the Lord has turned against me and become my enemy. All I wanted was some hope, Jonathan! Is there anything wrong with that?"

Everything in the way he sought it. "And did Samuel offer you any?" Jonathan knew better.

"He said the Lord has done what he predicted and torn the kingdom from me, giving it to one of my rivals—to *David*!" Saul rocked back and forth, his face ashen. "All because I didn't obey the Lord and carry out God's anger

against the Amalekites. The Lord will hand us over to the
Philistines. I will die tomorrow. I will die and so will—"
he groaned, pressing the heels of his hands into his eyes—
"my sons! *My sons!*"

After the first sharp, hot stab of fear, calmness came
over Jonathan. *So be it, Lord. Your will be done.* His father
had waged war against God, and his entire family would
bear the consequences.

Jonathan felt a stillness inside himself. Perhaps he had
known all along in the deepest recesses of his heart that he
too had to die, before David could become king. For if he
survived his father, there would always be those in
Benjamin, like Abner, who would want him to fight to
keep the crown. Even if he swore allegiance to David, the
struggle would go on and on.

Saul wailed. "What have I done? *What have I done?*" He
fell to the ground and wept bitterly. "My sons will die and
the blame must be laid upon my head. If I could live my
life over, I would—"

"Get up, Father." The time for self-recrimination was
over. Dawn approached. The enemy would not wait. "I
will help you put on your armor. We will go out and face
the Philistines together. And may God yet show mercy
upon us."

God promised to show mercy to a thousand generations
to those who loved the Lord. *God, dare I hope You will
bless my son? Please, protect him. Keep him out of the
clutches of evil men.*

"You will go with me?" Saul's eyes were wide with
fear. "Even after what I've done?"

"I will not abandon you. Have I not always honored
you as a son should honor his father?"

"And I have brought you to this." Tears glistened in Saul's eyes.

Jonathan gave him a hand up. "I will be where I belong, fighting at your side!"

He lifted his father's armor and helped him strap on the breastplate. When the king was ready, they went out together. Abner and the other commanders waited, faces grim.

Jonathan saw his brothers among them, fine men of valor. His throat tightened at the knowledge that they would die today. All of them, except the youngest who was safe in Gibeah. But safe for how long?

The king's armor bearer came forward and bowed low. "I was not summoned."

"My son Jonathan assisted me. Take your place beside me." The young man took up two shields and stood ready.

The battle lines were drawn. A great horde of Philistines filled the horizon, and their battle cry rose.

Jonathan turned, clinging to one last hope. "Abner! What word of David?"

"He is no longer with the Philistines."

Jonathan met his father's gaze and saw a waking world in Saul's eyes. Was he remembering the horde of Philistines they faced so many years ago and the boy who had rallied Israel's courage with a sling and a stone? How different today would be with David on their side!

Saul gave a single nod.

Jonathan drew his sword and started his run into the valley of death.

The shofars were blown.

Men shouted war cries.

The earth shook as thousands poured down the hill-sides. The enemy came on like avengers lusting for blood.

Jonathan fired arrows until he had none left.

The sound of battle became deafening. Screams of pain. The crash of swords, iron shattering bronze. Wheels rolling. Horses galloping. The hiss of a thousand arrows.

Malkishua was the first of Saul's sons to fall, four arrows in his chest. Then Abinadab gave a cry of pain, struck in the thigh. An arrow through his right eye sent him backward into the dust.

Dying men shrieked in terror and were silenced by a sword. Jonathan shouted orders to retreat. The Israelites fled before the Philistines, many falling with arrows in their backs.

Philistines surged up Mount Gilboa. *"Kill the king! Kill Saul!"*

Saul shouted, "Guard me! Keep them back!"

Jonathan swung to the right and to the left. He parried and thrust, blocked and made an upward cut. But there were too many. Too many!

His father ran up the hill. Jonathan followed. Arrows rained down around him. Suddenly Jonathan felt a hard blow in his side. Then another in his left shoulder.

"Jonathan!" Saul shouted.

Jonathan tried to raise his sword, but his strength was gone. At first, he felt no pain, and then pain so terrible he couldn't move. Two more arrows struck him in the chest. His knees buckled.

"My son!" Saul screamed. "My son!" A sound of rage and despair.

Swaying, Jonathan dug the point of his sword into the earth, but he could not hold himself up. When another arrow hit him, he fell heavily, driving the arrows in deeper. He rasped for breath and tasted blood. He felt the earth and grass against his cheek. He couldn't lift his head. Darkness closed in around him.

Body tensing, Jonathan fought against death, his fingers digging into the soil.

David! *David!*

Lord, be with my friend when he receives the crown. Give him wisdom to rule Your people Israel!

Battle sounds muted.

Everything within him fixed upon a single spot of light in the darkness. Surrendering, Jonathan sighed, blood bubbling in his throat. Then he felt lifted and drawn back like an arrow fitted into a bronze bow.

Back . . .

Back . . .

Back . . .

And then release!

Pain vanished. Grief fell away. He burst into freedom. In the twinkling of an eye, he moved into glorious colors and sounds, past myriads of singing angels, straight and true to the mark set in heaven.

And then Jonathan stood there, astonished and overwhelmed with joy, as he was embraced by the True Prince, who ushered him into the presence of God.

AFTER the battle, the Philistines returned to Mount Gilboa and stripped the dead. When they found the bodies of Saul and his three sons, they cut off the king's head, removed his armor, and sent out messengers across the land to boast of victory. They displayed King Saul's armor in the temple of the Ashtoreths. His body and those of his sons hung as trophies on the walls of Beth-shan.

When the people of Jabesh-gilead heard what the Philistines had done to Saul, they remembered how he had saved them from King Nahash and the Ammonites years before. Their valiant men traveled by night and took Saul and his sons down, carrying the bodies back to Jabesh, where they placed them on funeral pyres.

One item was removed from Jonathan's body before the fires were lit. Their remains were buried under a tamarisk tree at Jabesh, and the people fasted seven days to honor the dead.

Some were afraid of what David might do when he learned they had thus honored the former king. After all, Saul had been his enemy. Would David remember Jonathan as a friend and have mercy upon them?

They called for a volunteer to speak on their behalf.

"Take this to David. Perhaps he will remember his covenant of friendship with the king's son." The head of the elders' council gave the young man a small bundle wrapped in white linen. "All Israel knows that Prince Jonathan and David were best friends. May David honor the fallen prince and forgive any trespasses he sees against us. Go quickly! And may God be with you!"

The messenger headed south, traveling again through dangerous Philistine territory until he found David and his army in Ziklag.

Grim news had traveled quickly. An Amalekite had arrived the day before, boasting that he had taken the crown from Saul's head. David had had him executed.

Now, David mourned and ordered his followers to do the same.

Upon arriving at David's camp, the messenger insisted that he must speak with the king personally. The fate of Jabesh-gilead rested in David's hands.

A guard ushered the young man into David's presence.

The king of Judah raised his head. "I am told you are from Jabesh-gilead."

"I bring you news, my lord."

David's eyes darkened. "Better news than what I heard yesterday, I hope."

The young messenger bowed his head. "King Saul and his sons no longer hang on the walls of Beth-shan, my lord. Our warriors retrieved the bodies, and we have given them an honorable burial for rescuing our city from the Ammonites. I bring you this." He held out the parcel. "It belonged to your friend Prince Jonathan. No other should have it."

One of the guards took the small package and brought it to David.

David untied the leather cords and unrolled the cloth. His face contorted with grief, and tears streamed down his cheeks. "The Law." He held the scroll Jonathan had written and carried with him through the years. Worn from daily reading, stained with Jonathan's blood, it revealed to all the man he had been.

King Saul had pursued David across the land, driving him from place to place, but not once had Jonathan raised a hand against David! Instead, he had remained behind, holding the tribes together so they might stand firm against their common enemy: the Philistines. In obedience to the Law, Jonathan had honored his father and died beside him on Mount Gilboa.

David rolled the scroll carefully and placed it back in its torn leather casing. He drew the loop over his head and tucked the scroll inside his tunic against his heart. "Never did a man have a truer friend!"

That night, David wrote a song to honor Jonathan and King Saul.

> *Your pride and joy, O Israel, lies dead on the hills!*
> *Oh, how the mighty heroes have fallen! . . .*
> *How beloved and gracious were Saul and Jonathan!*
> *They were together in life and in death.*
> *They were swifter than eagles,*
> *stronger than lions. . . .*
> *Oh, how the mighty heroes have fallen in battle!*
> *Jonathan lies dead on the hills.*
> *How I weep for you, my brother Jonathan!*

David ordered all the men of Judah to learn the "Song of the Bow." It was sung for years to come.

David kept his promise to Jonathan. Although nearly all of Saul's grandsons were executed, one survived: Jonathan's only son, Merib-baal, also known as Mephibosheth. Crippled when his nurse fell upon him during the flight from Gibeah, he was kept hidden until David found him and took him into his household, where he lived out his life as an honored guest of the king.

An even greater promise was kept, too—one from the Lord God of Israel, who said in the Law that He would lavish love for generations to come upon those who loved Him: From Mephibosheth came many descendants, and like Jonathan, they became mighty warriors, renowned as experts with the bow.

DEAR READER,

You have just finished reading the poignant story of Jonathan, prince of Israel, by Francine Rivers. As always, it is Francine's desire for you the reader to delve into God's Word for yourself and discover the real story of Jonathan.

Jonathan's legacy was faithfulness. He was obedient to God at all costs, a loyal servant and regent of Israel. He was a trustworthy friend, an honorable son, and a protective father. He willingly accepted the course God charted for him and embraced his faith with all his might.

May God bless you as you discover the course He has laid out for you. May you willingly embrace it and find your legacy in Him.

Peggy Lynch

SEEK GOD'S WORD FOR TRUTH
Read the following passage:

"But when you were afraid of Nahash, the king of Ammon, you came to me and said that you wanted a king to reign over you, even though the LORD your God was already your king. All right, here is the king you have chosen. You asked for him, and the LORD has granted your request.

Now if you fear and worship the LORD and listen to his voice, and if you do not rebel against the LORD's commands, then both you and your king will show that you recognize the LORD as your God. But if you rebel against the LORD's commands and refuse to listen to him, then his hand will be as heavy upon you as it was upon your ancestors.

"As for me, I will certainly not sin against the LORD by ending my prayers for you. And I will continue to teach you what is good and right. But be sure to fear the LORD and faithfully serve him. Think of all the wonderful things he has done for you. But if you continue to sin, you and your king will be swept away."

Saul was thirty years old when he became king, and he reigned for forty-two years. Saul selected 3,000 special troops from the army of Israel and sent the rest of the men home. He took 2,000 of the chosen men with him to Micmash and the hill country of Bethel. The other 1,000 went with Saul's son Jonathan to Gibeah in the land of Benjamin.

Soon after this, Jonathan attacked and defeated the garrison of Philistines at Geba. The news spread quickly among the Philistines. So Saul blew the ram's horn throughout the land, saying, "Hebrews, hear this! Rise up in revolt!" All Israel heard the news that Saul had destroyed the Philistine garrison at Geba and that the Philistines now hated the Israelites more than ever. So the entire Israelite army was summoned to join Saul at Gilgal.

The Philistines mustered a mighty army of 3,000 chariots, 6,000 charioteers, and as many warriors as the grains of sand on the seashore! They camped at Micmash east of Beth-aven. The men of Israel saw what a tight spot they were in; and because they were hard pressed by the enemy, they tried to hide in caves, thickets, rocks, holes, and cisterns. Some of them crossed the Jordan River and escaped into the land of Gad and Gilead.

Meanwhile, Saul stayed at Gilgal, and his men were trembling with fear. Saul waited there seven days for Samuel, as Samuel had instructed him earlier, but Samuel still didn't come. Saul realized that his troops were rapidly slipping away. So he demanded, "Bring me the burnt offering and the peace offerings!" And Saul sacrificed the burnt offering himself.

Just as Saul was finishing with the burnt offering, Samuel arrived. Saul went out to meet and welcome him, but Samuel said, "What is this you have done?"

Saul replied, "I saw my men scattering from me, and you didn't arrive when you said you would, and the Philistines are at Micmash ready for battle. So I said, 'The Philistines are ready to march against us at Gilgal, and I haven't even asked for the LORD's help!' So I felt compelled to offer the burnt offering myself before you came."

"How foolish!" Samuel exclaimed. "You have not kept the command the LORD your God gave you. Had you kept it, the LORD would have established your kingdom over Israel forever. But now your kingdom must end, for the LORD has sought out a man after his own heart. The LORD has already appointed him to be the leader of his people, because you have not kept the LORD's command."   1 SAMUEL 12:12-15, 23-25; 13:1-14

List the warnings Samuel proclaimed at Saul's coronation.

Who else besides Saul would have heard these admonitions?

What actions did Saul take?

What did Samuel tell him? List the specifics.

How would this affect Saul's son Jonathan?

What effect might information like this have had on Jonathan's attitude toward God? toward his father?

FIND GOD'S WAYS FOR YOU

Think of someone you admired who made poor choices that affected you and your future. What was the outcome?

What was (or is) your attitude toward this person? toward God?

> Those who listen to instruction will prosper; those who trust the LORD will be joyful.   PROVERBS 16:20

What advice is offered in this verse?

STOP AND PONDER

> Be careful how you live. Don't live like fools, but like those who are wise. Make the most of every opportunity in these evil days. Don't act thoughtlessly, but understand what the Lord wants you to do. Don't be drunk with wine, because that will ruin your life. Instead, be filled with the Holy Spirit.   EPHESIANS 5:15-18

SEEK GOD'S WORD FOR TRUTH
Read the following passage:

One day Jonathan said to his armor bearer, "Come on, let's go over to where the Philistines have their outpost." But Jonathan did not tell his father what he was doing.

Meanwhile, Saul and his 600 men were camped on the outskirts of Gibeah, around the pomegranate tree at Migron. Among Saul's men was Ahijah the priest, who was wearing the ephod, the priestly vest. Ahijah was the son of Ichabod's brother Ahitub, son of Phinehas, son of Eli, the priest of the LORD who had served at Shiloh.

No one realized that Jonathan had left the Israelite camp. To reach the Philistine outpost, Jonathan had to go down between two rocky cliffs that were called Bozez and Seneh. The cliff on the north was in front of Micmash, and the one on the south was in front of Geba. "Let's go across to the outpost of those pagans," Jonathan said to his armor bearer. "Perhaps the LORD will help us, for nothing can hinder the LORD. He can win a battle whether he has many warriors or only a few!"

"Do what you think is best," the armor bearer replied. "I'm with you completely, whatever you decide."

"All right then," Jonathan told him. "We will cross over and let them see us. If they say to us, 'Stay where you are or we'll kill you,' then we will stop and not go up to them. But if they say, 'Come on up and fight,' then we will go up. That will be the LORD's sign that he will help us defeat them."

When the Philistines saw them coming, they shouted, "Look! The Hebrews are crawling out of their holes!" Then the men from the outpost shouted to Jonathan, "Come on up here, and we'll teach you a lesson!"

"Come on, climb right behind me," Jonathan said to his armor bearer, "for the LORD will help us defeat them!"

So they climbed up using both hands and feet, and the Philistines fell before Jonathan, and his armor bearer killed those who came behind them. They killed some twenty men in all, and their bodies were scattered over about half an acre.

Suddenly, panic broke out in the Philistine army, both in the camp and in the field, including even the outposts and raiding parties. And just then an earthquake struck, and everyone was terrified.

Saul's lookouts in Gibeah of Benjamin saw a strange sight—the vast army of Philistines began to melt away in every direction. "Call the roll and find out who's missing," Saul ordered. And when they checked, they found that Jonathan and his armor bearer were gone.

Then Saul shouted to Ahijah, "Bring the ephod here!" For at that time Ahijah was wearing the ephod in front of the Israelites. But while Saul was talking to the priest, the confusion in the Philistine camp grew louder and louder. So Saul said to the priest, "Never mind; let's get going!"

Then Saul and all his men rushed out to the battle and found the Philistines killing each other. There was terrible confusion everywhere. Even the Hebrews who had previously gone over to the Philistine army revolted and joined in with Saul, Jonathan, and the rest of the Israelites. Likewise, the men of Israel who were hiding in the hill country of Ephraim joined the chase when they saw the Philistines running away. So the LORD saved Israel that day, and the battle continued to rage even beyond Beth-aven.

1 SAMUEL 14:1-23

Describe what you learn about Jonathan from this passage.

Who or what was the source of Jonathan's daring feat?

How did God honor Jonathan's faith?

Where were Saul and the rest of the army? What were they doing?

What was Saul's reaction to the event? What did he do?

What did God do for all of Israel that day?

FIND GOD'S WAYS FOR YOU

Describe a time when you plunged ahead in your job, community, family, or other circle of influence to do something others thought was not possible. What was the outcome? Who or what motivated you?

Do you consider yourself a faithful servant? Why or why not?

> The name of the LORD is a strong fortress; the godly run to him and are safe.   PROVERBS 18:10

What does God offer those who run to Him?

STOP AND PONDER

> Jesus told them, "I tell you the truth, if you have faith and don't doubt, you can do things like this and much more. You can even say to this mountain, 'May you be lifted up and thrown into the sea,' and it will happen. You can pray for anything, and if you have faith, you will receive it."
>
> MATTHEW 21:21-22

SEEK GOD'S WORD FOR TRUTH
Read the following passage:

As Saul watched David go out to fight the Philistine, he asked Abner, the commander of his army, "Abner, whose son is this young man?"

"I really don't know," Abner declared.

"Well, find out who he is!" the king told him.

As soon as David returned from killing Goliath, Abner brought him to Saul with the Philistine's head still in his hand. "Tell me about your father, young man," Saul said.

And David replied, "His name is Jesse, and we live in Bethlehem."

After David had finished talking with Saul, he met Jonathan, the king's son. There was an immediate bond of love between them, and they became the best of friends. From that day on Saul kept David with him and wouldn't let him return home. And Jonathan made a solemn pact with David, because he loved him as he loved himself. Jonathan sealed the pact by taking off his robe and giving it to David, together with his tunic, sword, bow, and belt.

Whatever Saul asked David to do, David did it successfully. So Saul made him a commander over the men of war, an appointment that was welcomed by the people and Saul's officers alike.

When the victorious Israelite army was returning home after David had killed the Philistine, women from all the towns of Israel came out to meet King Saul. They sang and danced for joy with tambourines and cymbals. This was their song:

"Saul has killed his thousands,

and David his ten thousands!"

This made Saul very angry. "What's this?" he said. "They credit David with ten thousands and me with only thousands. Next they'll be making him their king!" So from that time on Saul kept a jealous eye on David.

Saul now urged his servants and his son Jonathan to assassinate David. But Jonathan, because of his close friendship with David, told him what his father was planning. "Tomorrow morning," he warned him, "you must find a hiding place out in the fields. I'll ask my father to go out there with me, and I'll talk to him about you. Then I'll tell you everything I can find out."

The next morning Jonathan spoke with his father about David, saying many good things about him. "The king must not sin against his servant David," Jonathan said. "He's never done anything to harm you. He has always helped you in any way he could. Have you forgotten about the time he risked his life to kill the Philistine giant and how the LORD brought a great victory to all Israel as a result? You were certainly happy about it then. Why should you murder an innocent man like David? There is no reason for it at all!"

So Saul listened to Jonathan and vowed, "As surely as the LORD lives, David will not be killed."

Afterward Jonathan called David and told him what had happened. Then he brought David to Saul, and David served in the court as before.   I SAMUEL 17:55–18:9; 19:1-7

What were the circumstances surrounding Jonathan's introduction to David?

What was Jonathan's response to David?

How did Saul react to David?

Discuss Jonathan's boldness in opposing his father on behalf of his friend.

List the considerations Jonathan laid out for his father regarding David. How effective was his approach?

FIND GOD'S WAYS FOR YOU
Share about a time when you experienced immediate friendship. Are you still close to that person?

Has one of your friendships ever created conflict with your family?
If so, what steps did you take to resolve the conflict? What was the
outcome?

> There are "friends" who destroy each other, but a real
> friend sticks closer than a brother.   PROVERBS 18:24

How would you define *friends* in this verse?

STOP AND PONDER

> Two people are better off than one, for they can help each
> other succeed. If one person falls, the other can reach out
> and help. But someone who falls alone is in real trouble.
> Likewise, two people lying close together can keep each
> other warm. But how can one be warm alone? A person
> standing alone can be attacked and defeated, but two can
> stand back-to-back and conquer. Three are even better, for
> a triple-braided cord is not easily broken.
>   ECCLESIASTES 4:9-12

SEEK GOD'S WORD FOR TRUTH
Reread the following passage that was covered in the last study:

> Saul now urged his servants and his son Jonathan to assassi-
> nate David. But Jonathan, because of his close friendship
> with David, told him what his father was planning. "Tomor-
> row morning," he warned him, "you must find a hiding
> place out in the fields. I'll ask my father to go out there
> with me, and I'll talk to him about you. Then I'll tell you
> everything I can find out."
>
> The next morning Jonathan spoke with his father about
> David, saying many good things about him. "The king must
> not sin against his servant David," Jonathan said. "He's never
> done anything to harm you. He has always helped you in any
> way he could. Have you forgotten about the time he risked his
> life to kill the Philistine giant and how the LORD brought a
> great victory to all Israel as a result? You were certainly happy
> about it then. Why should you murder an innocent man like
> David? There is no reason for it at all!"
>
> So Saul listened to Jonathan and vowed, "As surely as the
> LORD lives, David will not be killed."
>
> Afterward Jonathan called David and told him what had
> happened. Then he brought David to Saul, and David
> served in the court as before.   1 SAMUEL 19:1-7

In this passage, what leadership skills and attributes does Jonathan exhibit?

Read the following passage:

> Now the men of Israel were pressed to exhaustion that day, because Saul had placed them under an oath, saying, "Let a curse fall on anyone who eats before evening—before I have full revenge on my enemies." So no one ate anything all day, even though they had all found honeycomb on the ground in the forest. They didn't dare touch the honey because they all feared the oath they had taken.
>
> But Jonathan had not heard his father's command, and he dipped the end of his stick into a piece of honeycomb and ate the honey. After he had eaten it, he felt refreshed. But one of the men saw him and said, "Your father made the army take a strict oath that anyone who eats food today will be cursed. That is why everyone is weary and faint."
>
> "My father has made trouble for us all!" Jonathan exclaimed. "A command like that only hurts us. See how refreshed I am now that I have eaten this little bit of honey. If the men had been allowed to eat freely from the food they found among our enemies, think how many more Philistines we could have killed!"
>
> Then Saul said, "Let's chase the Philistines all night and plunder them until sunrise. Let's destroy every last one of them."
>
> His men replied, "We'll do whatever you think is best."
>
> But the priest said, "Let's ask God first."
>
> So Saul asked God, "Should we go after the Philistines? Will you help us defeat them?" But God made no reply that day.
>
> Then Saul said to the leaders, "Something's wrong! I want all my army commanders to come here. We must find out what sin was committed today. I vow by the name of the LORD who rescued Israel that the sinner will surely die, even if it is my own son Jonathan!" But no one would tell him what the trouble was.
>
> Then Saul said, "Jonathan and I will stand over here, and all of you stand over there."
>
> And the people responded to Saul, "Whatever you think is best."

Then Saul prayed, "O LORD, God of Israel, please show us who is guilty and who is innocent." Then they cast sacred lots, and Jonathan and Saul were chosen as the guilty ones, and the people were declared innocent.

Then Saul said, "Now cast lots again and choose between me and Jonathan." And Jonathan was shown to be the guilty one.

"Tell me what you have done," Saul demanded of Jonathan.

"I tasted a little honey," Jonathan admitted. "It was only a little bit on the end of my stick. Does that deserve death?"

"Yes, Jonathan," Saul said, "you must die! May God strike me and even kill me if you do not die for this."

But the people broke in and said to Saul, "Jonathan has won this great victory for Israel. Should he die? Far from it! As surely as the LORD lives, not one hair on his head will be touched, for God helped him do a great deed today." So the people rescued Jonathan, and he was not put to death.

Then Saul called back the army from chasing the Philistines, and the Philistines returned home.

1 SAMUEL 14:24-30, 36-46

What do we learn about Jonathan's leadership abilities from this passage?

Contrast Jonathan's relationship with the people to his father's.

Compare Jonathan and Saul regarding wisdom and logic.

Of what value was Jonathan to his father?

How did the people value Jonathan? How did they show it?

FIND GOD'S WAYS FOR YOU
How do your peers perceive you? What about those in authority over you?

What leadership skills do you have? Have you made them available to God?

Search me, O God, and know my heart; test me and know
my anxious thoughts. Point out anything in me that offends
you, and lead me along the path of everlasting life.

PSALM 139:23-24

How do you think God will measure your abilities?

STOP AND PONDER

A person who is put in charge as a manager must be faithful. As for me [the apostle Paul], it matters very little how
I might be evaluated by you or by any human authority. I
don't even trust my own judgment on this point. My con-
science is clear, but that doesn't prove I'm right. It is the
Lord himself who will examine me and decide.

1 CORINTHIANS 4:2-4

SEEK GOD'S WORD FOR TRUTH
Read the following passage:

David now fled from Naioth in Ramah and found Jonathan. "What have I done?" he exclaimed. "What is my crime? How have I offended your father that he is so determined to kill me?"

"That's not true!" Jonathan protested. "You're not going to die. He always tells me everything he's going to do, even the little things. I know my father wouldn't hide something like this from me. It just isn't so!"

Then David took an oath before Jonathan and said, "Your father knows perfectly well about our friendship, so he has said to himself, 'I won't tell Jonathan—why should I hurt him?' But I swear to you that I am only a step away from death! I swear it by the LORD and by your own soul!"

"Tell me what I can do to help you," Jonathan exclaimed.

David replied, "Tomorrow we celebrate the new moon festival. I've always eaten with the king on this occasion, but tomorrow I'll hide in the field and stay there until the evening of the third day. If your father asks where I am, tell him I asked permission to go home to Bethlehem for an annual family sacrifice. If he says, 'Fine!' you will know all is well. But if he is angry and loses his temper, you will know he is determined to kill me. Show me this loyalty as my sworn friend—for we made a solemn pact before the LORD—or kill me yourself if I have sinned against your father. But please don't betray me to him!"

"Never!" Jonathan exclaimed. "You know that if I had the slightest notion my father was planning to kill you, I would tell you at once."

Then David asked, "How will I know whether or not your father is angry?"

"Come out to the field with me," Jonathan replied. And

they went out there together. Then Jonathan told David, "I promise by the LORD, the God of Israel, that by this time tomorrow, or the next day at the latest, I will talk to my father and let you know at once how he feels about you. If he speaks favorably about you, I will let you know. But if he is angry and wants you killed, may the LORD strike me and even kill me if I don't warn you so you can escape and live. May the LORD be with you as he used to be with my father. And may you treat me with the faithful love of the Lord as long as I live. But if I die, treat my family with this faithful love, even when the LORD destroys all your enemies from the face of the earth."

So Jonathan made a solemn pact with David, saying, "May the LORD destroy all your enemies!" And Jonathan made David reaffirm his vow of friendship again, for Jonathan loved David as he loved himself.

Then Jonathan said, "Tomorrow we celebrate the new moon festival. You will be missed when your place at the table is empty. The day after tomorrow, toward evening, go to the place where you hid before, and wait there by the stone pile. I will come out and shoot three arrows to the side of the stone pile as though I were shooting at a target. Then I will send a boy to bring the arrows back. If you hear me tell him, 'They're on this side,' then you will know, as surely as the LORD lives, that all is well, and there is no trouble. But if I tell him, 'Go farther—the arrows are still ahead of you,' then it will mean that you must leave immediately, for the LORD is sending you away. And may the LORD make us keep our promises to each other, for he has witnessed them."

So David hid himself in the field, and when the new moon festival began, the king sat down to eat. He sat at his usual place against the wall, with Jonathan sitting opposite him and Abner beside him. But David's place was empty. Saul didn't say anything about it that day, for he said to himself, "Something must have made David ceremonially unclean." But when David's place was empty again the next day, Saul asked

Jonathan, "Why hasn't the son of Jesse been here for the meal either yesterday or today?"

Jonathan replied, "David earnestly asked me if he could go to Bethlehem. He said, 'Please let me go, for we are having a family sacrifice. My brother demanded that I be there. So please let me get away to see my brothers.' That's why he isn't here at the king's table."

Saul boiled with rage at Jonathan. "You stupid son of a whore!" he swore at him. "Do you think I don't know that you want him to be king in your place, shaming yourself and your mother? As long as that son of Jesse is alive, you'll never be king. Now go and get him so I can kill him!"

"But why should he be put to death?" Jonathan asked his father. "What has he done?"

Then Saul hurled his spear at Jonathan, intending to kill him. So at last Jonathan realized that his father was really determined to kill David.

Jonathan left the table in fierce anger and refused to eat on that second day of the festival, for he was crushed by his father's shameful behavior toward David.

The next morning, as agreed, Jonathan went out into the field and took a young boy with him to gather his arrows. "Start running," he told the boy, "so you can find the arrows as I shoot them." So the boy ran, and Jonathan shot an arrow beyond him. When the boy had almost reached the arrow, Jonathan shouted, "The arrow is still ahead of you. Hurry, hurry, don't wait." So the boy quickly gathered up the arrows and ran back to his master. He, of course, suspected nothing; only Jonathan and David understood the signal. Then Jonathan gave his bow and arrows to the boy and told him to take them back to town.

As soon as the boy was gone, David came out from where he had been hiding near the stone pile. Then David bowed three times to Jonathan with his face to the ground. Both of them were in tears as they embraced each other and said good-bye, especially David.

At last Jonathan said to David, "Go in peace, for we have

sworn loyalty to each other in the LORD's name. The LORD is
the witness of a bond between us and our children forever."
Then David left, and Jonathan returned to the town.

                                                    1 SAMUEL 20:1-42

What is Jonathan's first response to David's accusations regarding
his father?

What does Jonathan's oath imply?

Jonathan took his usual approach with his father regarding David.
What happened this time?

Do you think Jonathan believed his father was capable of murdering David? Why or why not?

What convinced Jonathan?

Upon hearing the outcome of Jonathan's confrontation with his father, David fled. What did Jonathan do?

FIND GOD'S WAYS FOR YOU
Do you believe the best about your parents? Why or why not?

Have you ever gone against your parents' wishes? If so, what happened? If not, why not?

My child, listen when your father corrects you. Don't
neglect your mother's instruction. What you learn from
them will crown you with grace and be a chain of honor
around your neck.   PROVERBS 1:8-9

What does God promise to those who obey their parents' teaching?

STOP AND PONDER

Dear children, remain in fellowship with Christ so that
when he returns, you will be full of courage and not shrink
back from him in shame. Since we know that Christ is righteous, we also know that all who do what is right are God's
children.   1 JOHN 2:28-29

SEEK GOD'S WORD FOR TRUTH
Review 1 Samuel 20:1-42 (printed at the beginning of the previous chapter). What arrangements did Jonathan make for his family?

Who was he trusting to see that the arrangements were carried out?

Read the following passages:

> Now the Philistines attacked Israel, and the men of Israel fled before them. Many were slaughtered on the slopes of Mount Gilboa. The Philistines closed in on Saul and his sons, and they killed three of his sons—Jonathan, Abinadab, and Malkishua. The fighting grew very fierce around Saul, and the Philistine archers caught up with him and wounded him severely.
>
> Saul groaned to his armor bearer, "Take your sword and kill me before these pagan Philistines come to run me through and taunt and torture me."
>
> But his armor bearer was afraid and would not do it. So Saul took his own sword and fell on it. When his armor bearer realized that Saul was dead, he fell on his own sword and died beside the king. So Saul, his three sons, his armor bearer, and his troops all died together that same day.

When the Israelites on the other side of the Jezreel Valley
and beyond the Jordan saw that the Israelite army had fled
and that Saul and his sons were dead, they abandoned their
towns and fled. So the Philistines moved in and occupied
their towns.   1 SAMUEL 31:1-7

Then David composed a funeral song for Saul and Jonathan,
and he commanded that it be taught to the people of Judah.
It is known as the Song of the Bow, and it is recorded in *The
Book of Jashar*.

"Your pride and joy, O Israel, lies dead on the hills!
  Oh, how the mighty heroes have fallen!
  Don't announce the news in Gath,
  don't proclaim it in the streets of Ashkelon,
  or the daughters of the Philistines will rejoice
  and the pagans will laugh in triumph.
  O mountains of Gilboa,
  let there be no dew or rain upon you,
  nor fruitful fields producing offerings of grain.
  For there the shield of the mighty heroes was defiled;
  the shield of Saul will no longer be anointed with oil.
  The bow of Jonathan was powerful,
  and the sword of Saul did its mighty work.
  They shed the blood of their enemies
  and pierced the bodies of mighty heroes.
  How beloved and gracious were Saul and Jonathan!
  They were together in life and in death.
  They were swifter than eagles,
  stronger than lions.
  O women of Israel, weep for Saul,
  for he dressed you in luxurious scarlet clothing,
  in garments decorated with gold.
  Oh, how the mighty heroes have fallen in battle!
  Jonathan lies dead on the hills.
  How I weep for you, my brother Jonathan!
  Oh, how much I loved you!

> And your love for me was deep,
> deeper than the love of women!
> Oh, how the mighty heroes have fallen!
> Stripped of their weapons, they lie dead." 2 SAMUEL 1:17-27

How—and with whom—did Jonathan die?

What did the people of Israel do after Saul and Jonathan were killed?

How did David honor his covenant with Jonathan?

Discuss David's tribute to Jonathan.

FIND GOD'S WAYS FOR YOU

What arrangements have you made for those you love after you die?

What kind of legacy will you leave?

> A good reputation is more valuable than costly perfume.
> And the day you die is better than the day you are born.
>
> ECCLESIASTES 7:1

What do you think your dearest friends will say about you when you are gone?

STOP AND PONDER

Because we are united with Christ, we have received an
inheritance from God, for he chose us in advance, and he
makes everything work out according to his plan. When
you believed in Christ, he identified you as his own by giving you the Holy Spirit, whom he promised long ago. The
Spirit is God's guarantee that he will give us the inheritance
he promised and that he has purchased us to be his own
people.   EPHESIANS 1:11, 13-14

Jonathan was a prince, a fine son, a loving friend, a caring father. And as a leader, he was a selfless servant. His life whispers of another Prince—a fine Son, a loving Friend, a caring Leader, and a selfless Servant: Jesus.

Let Jesus' words penetrate your heart and provide your legacy:

> I have loved you even as the Father has loved me. Remain in my love. When you obey my commandments, you remain in my love, just as I obey my Father's commandments and remain in his love. I have told you these things so that you will be filled with my joy. Yes, your joy will overflow! This is my commandment: Love each other in the same way I have loved you. There is no greater love than to lay down one's life for one's friends. You are my friends if you do what I command. I no longer call you slaves, because a master doesn't confide in his slaves. Now you are my friends, since I have told you everything the Father told me. You didn't choose me. I chose you. I appointed you to go and produce lasting fruit, so that the Father will give you whatever you ask for, using my name. This is my command: Love each other.   JOHN 15:9-17

FRANCINE RIVERS has been writing for almost thirty years. From 1976 to 1985 she had a successful writing career in the general market and won numerous awards. After becoming a born-again Christian in 1986, Francine wrote *Redeeming Love* as her statement of faith.

Since then, Francine has published numerous books in the CBA market and has continued to win both industry acclaim and reader loyalty. Her novel *The Last Sin Eater* won the ECPA Gold Medallion, and three of her books have won the prestigious Romance Writers of America RITA Award.

Francine says she uses her writing to draw closer to the Lord, that through her work she might worship and praise Jesus for all He has done and is doing in her life.

BOOKS BY BELOVED AUTHOR
FRANCINE RIVERS

OVER 2.5 MILLION SOLD!

Visit www. francinerivers.com

Visit us at tyndalefiction.com

Check out the latest information on your

favorite fiction authors and upcoming new

books! While you're there, don't forget to

register to receive *Fiction First*, our e-newsletter

that will keep you up to date on all of

Tyndale's Fiction.